GOOD MORNING,

MR. DALTON

(A Novella)

by Ana Shapkaliska

Ebook formatting by Rebecca Dalton at www.RebeccaDalton.net. Cover design by James at www.GoOnWrite.com.

EBOOK EDITION | 978-1-7330640-0-2
PAPERBACK EDITION | 978-1-7330640-1-9

This book is dedicated to Mr. A. Dalton

DAFINA

I'M DRIVING BACK HOME TO Cary. I just spent a few unforgettable hours with my lover in a nice hotel in Raleigh. Not the most expensive, not the cheapest. We always choose the golden middle. I don't want him to get ripped off.

He's the only reason I'm still in North Carolina. Before we fell for each other, I was seriously considering moving to NYC for good. As a writer seeking my first big break, I should really be in New York.

I feel so isolated in Cary, like I'm just wasting my time. My good friends have told me hundreds of times that I'm in the worst possible place for my career.

They're right.

But my love, Alec, is here. So, I'm here too.

Christians believe that heaven is above everything. For a very long time, I believed that too. But now I know that there is something above heaven. And that's when our two bodies get together and become one. And that's when we talk. And laugh.

And hold hands. And support each other's dreams.

We meet once a month. We'd both like to see each other more often, but for us that's not possible. I'm a married woman with two stepchildren. He is a married man with three children.

Our lovemaking always happens in the same order. He gently kisses my lips and face, then I feel his tongue in my mouth. We kiss for a long time and don't want to stop.

After that, he kisses my breasts. Nobody has ever kissed them so wonderfully as my gorgeous boyfriend.

Then I'm licking and sucking his intimate parts. After that, he penetrates me, lying on top of me.

The pleasure of being together increases every time, both emotionally and bodily. There are no words to describe how phenomenal it feels.

He is my piece of paradise in the darkness of North Carolina.

He always tells me I'm the best lover he's ever had, that I'm his true soulmate. And the way he looks at me, I believe him.

I'm always telling him I love his body, his smell, his flavor, but even more than that, his soul. And the way I look at him, he believes me too.

Our encounters give me strength for everything else in my life.

Not only for my writing, which is my heart and soul, but also for going to Broadway shows when they come to town, for listening to Beethoven and Chopin, or for wandering hours and hours through the museums.

His presence in my life gives me strength to

cook, to clean, to do the vacuuming and dusting, to scrub the floors in the kitchen and in the bathroom on my knees, to bring out the garbage.

Everybody says I'm a vivacious person. But having my love by my side makes me feel even more alive. With Alec, I feel like I can move mountains and make my dreams come true.

A suit and tie, sparks in the eyes, and a half-seductive smile. The man says, "You're my ride?"

I always feel the joy in a gentleman's voice. I never miss it. It's so strong.

On an average, I meet eight to nine new men every week. Some of them I bring to the airport. Some from the airport.

Every one of them, though, has his own unique story. His own unique suffering.

That's been my main job over the last few years. I've stopped counting in my notebook how many of them were in my car after I reached 594.

If I had continued counting, I believe the number would be more than 860.

Fortunately, I don't have a very good visual memory, and I easily forget faces. Otherwise, my dreams at night would be full of different men.

Mr. Dalton

My girlfriend Dafina is the most reclusive hermit on earth.

She never calls me, never e-mails me, never sends me texts.

I'm joking with her: "How am I going to reach you? Do I have to train some pigeons to bring you my letters in their beaks?"

She laughed at that for a long time. Tears came to her eyes, and she said her stomach ached.

Finally, she said: "That would be so cool. I like the idea very much."

Then she suddenly made a serious face.

"Look, Alec, you are too precious to me. I don't want to see you in any kind of trouble. I don't want even the most skillful detective on earth to be able to track us down ever. If we get caught, for me that would be a relief. You know, to break free. But for you, it would be bad news. Not because your marriage is perfect, but because of the children and the property. I don't want you to lose that big beautiful house. You're the one working so hard. In the year and a half since I first met you, how many times did I take you from your home to the airport and back? I don't even remember. But whenever you came back, every single time I could see the fatigue on your face. To me, even then you were handsome, because I knew you had done your job the best you could.

"Also, I don't want your children to resent you, and to remember you only when they need more money. Children can be very selfish and cruel. They always expect their parents to sacrifice everything for them.

"So, please my dearest, try to see me as someone who's not paranoid but protective. And there is a big difference."

MR. DALTON

YOU MUST WONDER HOW WE REACH EACH OTHER.

I honestly wondered that myself, when she told me it wasn't safe for me to be receiving calls from her.

So, I'd call her and after our conversation we'd both immediately erase the call.

One thing's for sure. When Dafina makes it big, the reporters will have trouble reaching her for an interview. She'll be hiding somewhere in Europe, or some beautiful temple in India.

Dafina is not on Facebook. Dafina is not on Twitter.

She used to have her profile on LinkedIn, but whoever tries to join her network, meets with rejection. She never accepts anybody. I'm not sure about the President of the United States or Bill Gates though. If they wanted to join her, maybe she would consider accepting them.

I love being with her. She makes me a happier,

better and stronger man. Those few hours that we spent together once a month, give me strength to sustain all the stress of my job, and all the burdens of my family life.

I have just one desire: for the beautiful feelings that this woman inspires in me to never fade away.

DAFINA

It's October 1998. I'm in Berlin attending one of the most prestigious TV festivals in Europe, "Prix Europa". The best of the best from the TV industry in Europe are assembled there.

I'm watching a lot of TV movies every day, some features, some documentaries. Some are real masterpieces. I'm amazed at the talent of the people who made them.

I feel good. It's good to be there again. Between the screenings, all the attendees gather in the hall.

Everybody is pretty dressed up. Whether casual or formal, they've chosen their clothes to impress. You can see the most expensive jeans and sneakers, suits and dresses.

I'm always dressed in different suits and long narrow skirts with slits, because it looks elegant and more feminine. The air in the hall smells of beautiful perfumes as well as of ambition, prestige, pride, doubts, anxiety and fear. Who is going to get the breakthrough? Who is going to be left behind?

Personally, I'm quite content with how my project went.

Besides all the amazing people at the festival, I made friends with a girl - the receptionist at the hotel where I'm staying. She is very interested in me in many ways. Whenever we meet, she asks about my job, my country.

Last evening, before my departure to Macedonia, she asked how old I was.

When I told her I was thirty-two, she was so shocked.

"You're thirty-two? Oh, you are so old, but you look so young!"

That was her goodbye to me.

I just smiled at her.

Then she asked: "What do you think, how old am I?"

She looked pretty much my age but to be polite I say twenty-five.

"I'm sixteen," she replies.

My time in Berlin was full of hard work but also hard play. I did have a lot of fun, I can't complain.

I'm going home with a lot of incredible stories in my heart and in my pockets.

It's October 2003. I'm travelling by bus to spend

part of my vacation with some close friends in Zagreb, the capital of Croatia. The fall is magnificent, and I'm enjoying the landscape, sitting by the window.

The bus attendant makes friends with me. We laugh and joke the whole ride. At one point he sees my ID and my age and is dumbstruck. He is completely appalled and shouts: "Dafina!"

I feel like a freak.

It's January 2010. Cary, North Carolina. I'm celebrating my birthday. About twenty-five people are in our tiny apartment. Everybody is relaxed and comfortable. They enjoy the home made dishes and live music that my close friends are performing specially for me.

Lucrecia is playing the guitar, Peggy the cello, and Jason is on the drums.

Among the other guests, there is a lesbian couple. Sharon has been my friend for years, and she brought her new lover, Stephanie, along. Stephanie's enjoying the party too. She admires the food: "I've never had such good food in my whole life."

She dances to the rhythm of the music, laughs and makes friends.

Later in the evening, she approaches me.

"May I ask you a personal question?"

"Sure, go ahead."

"How old are you?"

"Today, I turn forty-four."

She looks at me shocked and starts shouting: "No way! No way! No way!"

I'm flattered, but still uncomfortable because everybody turns to stare at me. I excuse myself and go in the other room to refresh my perfume.

Once, while giving Mr. Dalton a ride from the airport to his home in Fuquay-Varina, I mentioned how old I was, and he was very surprised. But being a refined gentleman, he didn't react in a way to make me blush. I thank him for that. He was relieved to hear my age, because he realized that the age difference between us was not inappropriate.

MR. DALTON

For someone so talented who has traveled half the world, I'd expected a little more creativity in her planning, but she set up our first date at the buffet of a fancy grocery store.

My first thought was: "Is she freaking kidding me? Is she ashamed to be seen in public with me? Where's her sense of romance? Like dinner with candles, champagne and live music, or kissing under the stars."

But after I gave it a second thought, it dawned on me that her idea was very creative.

It couldn't have been smarter. For two people who are married, that is one of the safest places to meet. Looks silly, but it's the smartest choice.

So that we can peacefully fix the date and time of our encounter in some hotel room, snacking over some freshly baked pastry and sipping our coffees. If somebody sees us together, we can always make a show that we had met accidentally.

Mr. Dalton: Hi, Dafina. How are you? So good to see you!

Dafina: Hello, Mr. Dalton. I'm good, thank you. I just came to get my favorite cookies and some chocolates.

Mr. Dalton: I'm getting some stuff too. How about grabbing a coffee together? Do you have a minute?

Dafina: Sure. I'd love to have coffee with you, Mr. Dalton.

Mr. Dalton: Such a gorgeous day today. Isn't it?

Dafina: It's a beautiful day, Mr. Dalton. Very beautiful.

DAFINA

Every day there are different men in my car.

One gentleman says into his phone as I'm bringing him to the airport: "A gorgeous girl came to pick me up."

I don't consider myself a good driver, and I bet all the gentlemen I drive are much better drivers than me, but somehow, they all seem pleased with my performance.

"It was a very pleasant ride."

"Thank you, sir."

There are three suits and three ties in my car. The gentleman in the passenger's seat says: "We like you very much. It was a great pleasure to sit next to you."

"Thank you, sir."

As he gives me a huge tip, I can't help but notice that he stinks of sweat.

I wonder: "Is there a lack of male deodorants in the store or what?"

Another gentleman: "I haven't had such a good ride in a long time. That was wonderful."

"Thank you, sir."

Another gentleman: "Have you ever done any modeling?"

"No sir, never."

Another gentleman: "Always a pleasure. I've been missing you, you know."

I keep quiet.

One strawberry blonde lady in her fifties: "You're like a bright ray of sunshine, so vivacious, so outgoing. I bet your customers enjoy riding with you."

"Thank you, ma'am."

A tired-looking CEO: "I've had such a difficult week, and an especially difficult day, but you made my day and my whole week too. Thank you so much."

"You're welcome, sir."

Another gentleman: "You are an excellent driver".

"Thank you, sir."

The gentleman keeps praising me throughout the whole ride, saying what an incredible driver I am, and then, at the end, gives me a five-percent tip.

Obviously, there's a lot of testosterone in my car. A lot.

To be totally honest, I never wanted to drive men. I was happy with my three ladies: Yvonne, Kimberly and Dotty. But the money I was making wasn't enough for our household. So, my husband started giving me more and more trips.

At first, I didn't feel comfortable driving men— no matter that most of them were CEOs or high-ranking executives— because deep down I'm very shy. But most of the men really do enjoy my company a great deal. Rarely, one of them feels awkward and shy too.

The gentlemen who are smarter and more in- sightful find this kind of job pretty incongruent for a lady like me. But I quickly explain that I'm just helping my husband in his business, when no- body else is available.

So, because of the needs of our household, I was exposed to so many men.

In the beginning I tried to refuse, telling my husband I didn't like men in my car. Most of them were flirting with me. Some of them even try to touch me. I kept quiet about the invitations for drinks.

It's flattering to hear: "You're so beautiful. You look great. You are stunning…" But when it goes like that all the time, it gets intense.

At the end of the day, I feel exhausted from all the racy vibes.

When I go home I take a shower, eat something that I cooked in the morning, and open up my laptop to the website: www.mayapur.tv

There's twenty-four hour programing, spiritual music and classes. That's the channel of the headquarters of my adopted religion, and it's based in Mayapur, West Bengal, India.

Being raised as an orthodox Christian, I've enjoyed a wonderful upgrade in learning more about God by studying the holy scriptures of India. In a way, I believe it has made me a better Christian.

Over the last three or four days, I haven't been feeling well. Lately, I've been working very hard and sleeping very little. All day long, I'm driving people. Half of the night I'm working on my book. It's my fifth.

I'm taking Tylenol three times a day and extra vitamin C. I can't eat much.

Still in that condition, I'm taking care of my regular customers without complaining. But my husband is trying to load me up with trips. When I refuse, he becomes furious. I can sense the dissatisfaction in his voice because I'm unable to drive as much as he expects me to and he is resentful.

HEMANT: But you like the airport trips the best. I'm giving you the best trips.

DAFINA: I do like them the best, but not 24/7. And not when I'm sick.

How come he doesn't even ask how I'm feeling before demanding that I go on these trips?

Now he's snoring like a train in the other room, as I'm writing this on the sofa.

Last night my body was burning with fever, but somehow he still expected me to give him sexual pleasure.

I've just humbly asked: "Please leave me alone. I'm really not feeling well."

LIDIA

I'M ONE OF DAFINA'S BEST FRIENDS. WE ARE VERY CLOSE and love each other deeply, in spite of being as different from each other as the earth and sky. Our outlook on life is completely opposite. It's a miracle we're so connected.

I know Dafina from our preschool days and we've been friends ever since. Even though she is ten thousand miles away from Skopje, I don't feel separated from her. She calls me often, and I know what's going on with her.

When her calls come after midnight, I immediately know she has something very important to share with me. I suffer from insomnia, so I don't mind her calling me so late.

Let me tell you an interesting story about her.

We were in sixth grade, and were going for summer holidays to the Croatian coast, in Dubrovnik. It was organized by our school. So, our parents were not with us.

After a few days there, we met some interesting high school boys on the beach from Zagreb, the Capitol of Croatia.

One boy fell in love with her. Somehow he came to know that sweets were her weakness. He intended to invite her on a date, and bought a huge, creamy, multilayer chocolate cake. He came to her with the cake, and begged her to go out with him.

Dafina liked the cake, but didn't like the boy. So, because of the boy, she refused the cake.

The phone is ringing. It's half past one in the morning. I see her name and know it's something that she badly wants to share.

First thing she tells me is: "I fell for a married guy."

"So what?" I reply. "As I remember, you are married too."

"Lidia, you're the only person I can talk to. You're not going to think I'm an impudent whore or a nasty criminal."

"Calm down, my dear. It happens all the time. If he's a married, he's not dead."

Dafina laughs.

"If you told me that you fell for a dead man, then I'd advise you to see a therapist. But with this news, I'm just happy for you. And I'm honored that you're calling to share your joy with me. How old is he, Dafina?"

"I've never asked him, but he once mentioned his sign in Chinese astrology, so I figured out that he's about six years older than me, and the same sign as my beloved niece. I see many similarities between them."

That's a beautiful age difference. It's important to have a good fuck, but even more important is to have a good talk."

DAFINA

SAM COLLINS AND KAZUO MURAKAMI ARE TWO VERY important people in my life. They are my beautiful gay friends. I find them to be extraordinarily smart and cool, and I love them deeply.

Sam is my age, mid-forties. He's tall, handsome and sexy, with tattoos all over his arms. He used to teach history of art at Stanford. Now he is doing his second PhD at Duke in anthropology. He lives in the apartment beneath us, which Mr. Murakami pays for.

He's divorced. His ex-wife and two children live in San Francisco.

Mr. Kazuo Murakami is a stunningly handsome man in his fifties. His captivating Japanese glance penetrates your heart and melts it right away. He is the CEO of a company whose headquarters are in Raleigh and Hong Kong. He is married with four children— two sons and two daughters. The sons live in Tokyo, and the daughters with Mr. Murakami and his wife Aiko in a huge mansion on

Giovanni Court up Regency Parkway in Cary.

Sam and Mr. Murakami are a real power couple. Sam is the creative force, and Mr. Murakami is the brain and the financial supporter.

I give them rides whenever they fly out of town, separately or together, and I pick them up on their return.

I also take care of Mr. Murakami's wife, Aiko, and his two daughters when they go on shopping sprees to Paris, Milan or Shanghai. Aiko loves me very much, and she opens her heart to me every time she sees me. Last time I picked her up, she told me that she would love to spend her final years in Shanghai because she feels a special connection to that place.

"I feel like I must have lived there in a previous lifetime. Many years ago, when I visited Shanghai for the first time, I felt like I'd been there before—everything looked so familiar to me. It felt like home."

The question about reincarnation is very personal to me, so I keep quiet. I don't feel comfortable discussing it with everybody.

Sam is my best friend in Cary. I love to talk to him about books, movies, music, and art. He always encourages me about my writing, and says that he has a strong feeling that I'm going to make it. His belief in me is so comforting. He's read all of my books that have been translated into English.

When my husband comes home late at night, tired and grumpy, I ask him: "Hemant, are you happy with me?"

He replies: "What?"

I repeat: "Are you happy with me? How come you never want to spend time with me? You never want to make time for me?"

He looks at me blankly: "What are you talking about?"

In return, I look at him blankly too. "Nothing, Hemant. Nothing important, I guess."

At least he's a real sweetheart when he wants to have sex. And that's something.

I always try to see the bright side. That's who I am.

SAM

It's FIVE IN THE MORNING. I'M LYING IN BED WITH THE love of my life, Kazuo. We can hear the music from Dafina's apartment. We look at each other and smile.

"Dafina is writing a new book, Kazuo."

Kazuo nods approvingly, and looks at me with that mesmerizing glance.

I'm taking the ear plugs from the drawer.

When we hear dancing on top of us, we immediately know what's going on—a new book is on the way. But she is a very considerate girl. When she writes, she gets up around three in the morning and has her first coffee. The music doesn't start until five.

"Her husband is never around," says Kazuo.

"Yes, our beautiful friend is like a white widow—married, but her husband is never by her side."

"She'll find her way. She is very clever."

"I feel the same, Kazuo. Dafina is always telling

me how she thanks God that Hemant came her way. Their relationship has given her so much material for stories and characters, and that's the most precious thing to her. Her attitude is that God always puts us in the situations that are the best for us."

"Such a good attitude. Pretty eastern though."

We put the ear plugs in and try to go back to sleep. We never tell her that she's waking us up in the middle of the night. We just love her the way she is.

DAFINA

To Mr. Robbins, I'm "darling."

To Mr. McPherson, I'm "sweetheart."

To Mr. Zimmerman, I'm "dear."

To Mr. Hills, I'm "babe."

To Mr. Anderson, I'm a movie freak.

"How come you always see the newest movies before anybody else? Are you sleeping in a movie theatre?"

To Mr. Donovan, I'm a chocolate addict. For some reason, he always catches me eating chocolate.

"Your car always smells like Belgian chocolate. Or Swiss chocolate. And perfumes."

I joke with him that life is easier with chocolates and perfumes. He smiles and agrees.

All these gentlemen prefer to sit in the front, next to me.

But Mr. Dalton has never asked if he could sit in the passenger's seat, and I like him even more because of that.

One morning I'm picking up an Indian gentleman from his hotel near my home, taking him to the company that he's visiting for one week. He's an IT guy, and I know him from before. He's handsome and has an open glance.

"You're still here, sir?"

"I went back to Chennai and came yesterday very late. It's always so good to see you. Always so refreshing. To see your eyes and smile, and hear your laughter. Can you please turn a little towards me, so I can enjoy your smile?"

I wanted to tell him: "Get the fuck out of my car, you moron," but I just say, "Thank you, sir. You made my day," and focus on my driving.

The same gentleman asks me the following morning to turn my face toward him again, so he can enjoy my beautiful glance. I feel awkward, but try my best to stay calm. He asks where I'm originally from, and he's delighted to hear that I'm Macedonian.

"Such an old culture and civilization!" He knows even that Macedonia is mentioned a few times in the Holy Bible.

So, he inquires further if I adopted the Indian lifestyle or my husband adopted the Macedonian.

I explain that I had been fascinated with the

ancient Indian culture known as Vedic culture long before I met my husband. Exactly fourteen years before we met, I started studying it passionately. That was already twenty-two years ago, and I've never stopped. So, for me that was nothing new or something I had to adjust to. I went on two long trips to India and traveled all around the country long before my husband came into picture.

I've read the Holy Scriptures of the Shrimad Bhagavatam (all eighteen cantos) three times, and the Chaitanya Charitamrita (nine thick cantos) four times.

In them, karma is so wonderfully explained.

The other day, Mr. Dalton mentioned to me that he believes in karma, and I was so delighted to hear that he knew about it too. Another thing that we share.

My husband has never read those Holy Scriptures, but he knows the stories because his mother read them to him when he was a child.

The flirtatious gentleman from Chennai suddenly noticed my earrings.

"Oh, you are wearing such big earrings. Are they heavy?"

"No, they're actually very light."

Without bothering to ask me, he grabs my right earring and feels it for himself.

I feel so humiliated.

I'm very happy that I never have to see him again after this trip. Somehow, he got removed from my life.

SAM

Long before Kazuo came into my life, things with my (now) ex-wife were rough. I didn't love her anymore. It was painful for me to face that, and I've struggled to admit it. But one day, I found redemption, and that was when I met Kazuo for the first time. It happened in Buenos Aires at a tango party. When our eyes met, I knew that I found my other half right then and there. By that time, I had already separated from my wife. Kazuo was with his wife, Aiko. I noticed the void between them immediately. They had such different energies. The moment I fell for Kazuo, Kazuo fell for me too.

I'm a very lucky man, because I found my true love.

It's not so painful anymore that my children have cut me off. I don't feel any resentment over that. My best friend from Cary, Dafina, tells me they'll come around some day. I wish them well, and pray they find the right path to become happier and better people.

Even in our happiest times as a family, I knew that children have their own life. As a parent I can guide them, help them, teach them, support them, but I can't protect them. One of my best friends from San Francisco is watching his daughter dying, right in front of his eyes. She's only twenty-eight and has lung cancer. She's never smoked in her life. He'll do whatever it takes to protect her from that horrible suffering, but her death is inevitable. He's helpless.

Ultimately, the children are on their own. And no parent has control over that.

I never had any regrets about my failed marriage. Dafina always makes my heart peaceful. There's a saying from her country: "Great love cannot be destroyed."

That's so true.

How can a love for somebody be so great, and yet fade away over time? It doesn't make any sense.

The same goes for friendship. As Dafina says: "Great friendship cannot be destroyed."

There are many people who have come into my life and disappeared. I don't lose my sleep over them anymore. If they left, they were supposed to be gone.

MR. DALTON

ACCORDING TO THE RULES IMPOSED BY DAFINA, WE never do ice cream and soda. We never do coffee and cookies. We never do lunch, dinner, movies, shows… We never show up together in public, except for the buffet at the fancy grocery store.

Dafina knows which hotels we can go to, and which we can't. And places where her husband and his co-workers might be dropping people off, she doesn't even mention.

The hotels where we meet are never in some isolated place. Instead, they must be near some shopping center with plenty of restaurants, movie theatres or bookstores.

We never park our cars in the same parking lot. We never enter or leave the hotel at the same time. She thinks about every single detail. She's always repeating that I'm too precious to her, that I'm the very best thing that has ever happened to her in North Carolina.

"If you are safe, I'm happy. If you are good, I'm peaceful."

She orchestrates our encounters joyfully, and I'm happy to follow along.

I've never met anybody who is so discreet and unselfish in my whole life.

I love talking to her. I love making love with her.

LIDIA

After she moved to the United States for good, in those first few days, Dafina discovered that her husband Hemant was completely broke. It was a huge shock for her. She knew that he had lost his job almost a year ago but thought that he was making good money with his trading business online.

It didn't turn out that way.

A few days went by, and then Hemant invited her on a ride through Cary. After driving around town for a while, they ended up at the Cary Town Center.

And instead of offering to treat her to something, or maybe spend a couple of hundred dollars on her, Hemant gives her dirty looks whenever she touches something that interests her.

Dafina: "What's the matter? You're making me feel very uncomfortable. I'm not asking you to buy me a purse for three thousand dollars. Or two-thousand-dollar shoes."

He would grumpily keep quiet.

Dafina picked up a purse for twenty-five dollars. He paid for it reluctantly and commented that he didn't like the bag.

When Hemant got fired from his job, he didn't tell anybody. Not even his two closest friends. Instead, he told them that he is working from home. Dafina was still in Macedonia, waiting for her green card, but she sensed that something weird was going on.

A couple of months later, he told his ex-wife that he had quit his job. This made her enraged. Now that he's got a new wife that he wants to impress, she thought, he isn't going to take proper care of the children. But instead of going to the child support agency and reporting that he had been laid off, he just paid the full child support for the next ten months, exhausting the last of his savings. But his ex-wife's envy over Dafina had already skyrocketed.

Dafina came to know about him being fired only six months later! He finally admitted what had happened, once her dad started inquiring about why it was taking forever to get the green card.

"Why didn't you tell me that you lost your job? I'm your wife. I'm supposed to know."

"I didn't want you to worry."

"I grew up in a family where my parents shared everything, good or bad," Dafina replied.

DAFINA

W<small>E KNEW EACH OTHER FOR MORE THAN A YEAR WHEN</small> we suddenly realized that we had fallen in love.

Looking back on it now, I see that it happened to both of us at the same time.

I felt his vibes. I felt his energy changing from being friendly to something more. I could hear the excited beating of his heart. I could even tell when he got slightly erect. I could feel the increased testosterone from the backseat.

I couldn't believe that such a beautiful person had fallen for me. I'm sure he felt the same way. Of all the men I drove, more than nine hundred of them, I wanted him and nobody else.

For a long time, I didn't want to admit my feelings for him. I fought very hard to suffocate them, to kill the desire to be with that man. When I would see the wedding ring on his left hand, I would scream at myself: "Put your foot on the brake, Dafina. Don't go forward. He is married, and for you that means: end of the program. He's someone's husband, someone's father, and I don't want anyone's feelings to get hurt."

His ring repulsed me immediately, cut off my desire.

Being raised in a rigid, religious family, I always judged my girlfriends whenever they fell for married guys and went out with them.

Like Lidia. I love her deeply, I really do, but I never approved of her always being someone's mistress. "Look at her," I'd say to myself. "She does everything wrong."

I knew she was going to support me, though, when I told her about Alec. My other girlfriends would tell me: "Stay away. Forget him." So, I wouldn't call them.

Since the time we were young, Lidia always told me that she preferred married men, because if she wanted to kick them out, they couldn't bother her. They're stuck. They couldn't make her life hell like the single men could.

Confession to myself: I love Mr. Dalton, but it's complex. On the one hand, it makes me feel invigorated and extraordinarily happy. But on the other, it makes me hate myself.

I've really fought hard to kick him out of my heart. I tried avoiding him, because I wanted so badly to forget him. And when my husband would tell me to pick him up, I'd say: "Send somebody else," or, "I'm busy, I'm tired, I'm not feeling well…" or, "I'll do some other trip…"

And even though I loved Mr. Dalton so much, I never look up his schedule. I never look in my husband's reservation book or computer to see when he will be flying.

When I used to work in the TV industry, a lot of powerful, married executives were very eager to be with me. I was single, creative, fun, and the best in my department. My projects always received better recognition than those of my colleagues. Every director, every producer wanted to work with me.

So, they'd invite me into their offices and offer me coffee or fruit juice. Some would offer cookies.

After talking about business, how things were going, and what was next on my agenda, they would very openly say that I was irresistible and that they wanted to get with me.

Instead of showing them that I was intimidated or uncomfortable, I'd put on my most seductive smile and say:

"No problem. Give me five thousand euros. I'll suck your dick."

Five thousand euros is a lot of money in Southern Europe, about seven and a half thousand US dollars.

I'd get up nonchalantly from my chair, leaving their mouths hanging open.

"So, when you're ready with the money, we'll talk about the time and place to fulfill your sexual desires."

In my real life, I've always avoided married guys. I didn't even find them attractive somehow.

I've never felt like taking advantage of a married boss or executive, to get ahead in my career.

If a guy already belongs to somebody else, fine. I'm not going to lose any sleep over him.

Just the opposite of Lidia, I didn't even find the married men as sexy as the single ones.

I run from them like a devil from the Holy Cross.

When I least expected it, though, I fell for Mr. Dalton. I never counted on that. I never would have predicted it.

I would never have opened up to him, if I wasn't positive, if I didn't feel so strongly that he had fallen for me too.

Being deeply religious, I do my prayers on my prayer beads for two hours every morning. But lately I've started getting up early, around two or three in the morning, after only few hours of sleep, to do extra prayers.

Somehow, I never felt that the Lord was angry with me for my heart getting captivated by Mr. Dalton. The way my husband has treated me emotionally all these years, my heart has become dry as an African desert.

I had prayed and prayed, diligently and honestly, for the Lord to show me the right path. I suffered deeply, because I didn't want to be in love with Mr. Dalton. I was even angry with myself.

But, despite all my prayers, my love for that gorgeous man only increased, instead of perishing, as I'd hoped.

For the first time in my six years in North Carolina, I went to the State Fair. I was just curious to see what was going on there.

I wanted to win a huge purple and pink Teddy Bear, so I had to pop a lot of balloons with darts. With every popped balloon I thought: just as this balloon disappears, let my love for Mr. Dalton vanish.

I'm very good at popping those balloons, so I won the Teddy Bear easily. The guy in charge was very pleased with me, and in addition to the bear, he gave me a beautiful rose made from polyester. The teddy bear I named Krishna, and the rose Radharani.

The truth is that neither the Lord nor the popped balloons helped me forget him.

For three months, I couldn't look Mr. Dalton in the eye. It was intense for me to sustain his glance, as it was full of longing for me. From light green, his eyes would become dark green. I felt so ashamed of myself too; I didn't want him to see the burning desire in my glances.

Finally, after three months of playing hide and seek, I looked back at him bravely and when he greeted me saying "Happy Monday," I replied audaciously, "Happy Monday to you, too."

All I can tell is that the desire for him is burning in my heart, and the longing is painful.

One part of me is dying to feel him on top of me, to feel him inside me. The other part prays for the hotel encounters never to happen.

Every single night, I fantasize about how we would make love, flying among the stars, among the different universes, and how we would reach spiritual heights…with him on top of me all along.

MR. DALTON

DAFINA WAS AFRAID I WOULD JUDGE HER WHEN SHE told me that she has only sent one text message in her whole life.

But what happened was just the opposite. I loved her even more.

Here's the story.

Usually on Saturdays she goes to the movie theatre. She spends the whole day there, watching three or four movies one after another. Sometimes even five. That's been her habit ever since her college days.

That Saturday, though, she didn't have the car. She had brought it the day before to the mechanic. So, in the morning, her husband gave her a ride to the theatre.

After watching four movies, she left the theatre at around ten in the evening and went to a nearby hotel. From the lobby, she called her husband and asked him politely if he can pick her up, because she was tired and hungry. He said he was at the airport and would be there in fifteen minutes. She felt relieved.

Well, time passed but there was no trace of Hemant.

After three hours, he finally showed up, apologizing for getting stuck with some ready to go trips, as well as with dispatching too.

Shortly before he arrived, my desperate girlfriend had tried her best to figure out how to send a text message and wrote him: "I'm starving".

That was before she had an iPhone, but a tiny flip phone.

She considers herself a dummy when it comes to electronics and technology. She says even toddlers are better than her in that respect.

"The technical side of my brain is not developed," she often jokes.

Being an executive in IBM and knowing a little something about technology, I'm like a demigod in her eyes. She admires me tremendously.

In my opinion, it would be scary if the technical side of her brain were as developed as the artistic side. There is no good book that she hasn't read, no good movie she hasn't seen. So, I find that charming. A good balance.

When I told her that my favorite subject has always been math, and that I was outstanding in that, she had admitted that she was the worst math student ever, and that math was her nightmare.

In Dafina's time, in Southern Europe, students were not free to choose their own subjects. So, math was mandatory in all four years of high school for everybody.

The first three years she went through hell with her math teacher. The lady was stern, and Dafina had to work extra hard not to flunk.

But in her senior year, a new math teacher came, an elderly lady who was a softhearted drunk, and Dafina saw the heaven with her. Usually math was at the end of the day. So, if they had five courses a day, the last one was math. For Dafina, that would mean only four courses. Or if they had four courses and the last one was math, for her that would mean just three. This was because she skipped the the math courses religiously.

At the end of the year, a classmate asked her: "Does the math teacher even know what you look like?"

"I don't think so," Dafina said.

While her classmates were sweating over math problems and tests, Dafina was watching movies in the theatre nearby. They used to give her popcorn and sodas for free all the time, because she was their best customer.

SAM

———————

DAFINA IS ALMOST FORTY-TWO AND THREE MONTHS
pregnant. She feels great: no morning sickness, no nau-
sea, no mood swings. Her spirit is light and her body's
even lighter. It's amazing for a woman her age. She tells
me she's never felt better or healthier in her whole life.

Hemant is still jobless. He's wasting more money with his online business than he's making. Still,
he pretends that he's very busy and doing well.

They struggle to put food on the table. When
she first moved from Europe, they used to cook
in the Hillsborough temple almost every Sunday.
After the program, they'd bring leftovers from the
feast and eat a little each day till the next Sunday.

One day they went to the Chinese grocery store
at the South Hills Shopping Center. The prices of
fruits and vegetables are much lower there than in
the other stores.

Dafina sees some beautiful pomegranates, one
of her favorite fruits, and went to take one.

As a pregnant woman, she has her cravings.

One pomegranate is two dollars.

Hemant sees her and scolds her: "Leave it, it's expensive."

So Dafina puts the pomegranate back.

I buy for her the things she likes, but not in a way to make her feel bad. She has her pride and never asks me for anything.

Kazuo loves her very much too, and often gets her gift cards for fancy stores.

So, she's pretty much very nicely dressed all the time.

I know what her favorite food is, and always make sure I have it at home, so we can share.

She's always very thankful.

She kisses me on the cheek and gives me a warm hug. Her belly has started to show, and she's getting chubbier in the face.

DAFINA

I'M NOT AN AMERICAN, AND I NEVER WILL BE.

    I don't have a tattoo.

    I never wear flip-flops.

    I don't like peanut butter and jelly sandwiches.

    I've never hit the gym.

LIDIA

HEMANT NEVER MENTIONED TO DAFINA THAT HIS younger brother was a severe schizophrenic. She discovered that on her own when she went to India the third time (the first time with her husband) for their Indian wedding.

It was the most magical wedding you could ever imagine.

It was performed at the ancient temple, Shri Shri Radha Damodar built during the fifteenth century in the holy town of Vrindavan. This town alone contains more than five thousand temples, and is about a two and a half hour car ride southeast of the capital city of Delhi. In that temple itself, Dafina's favorite spiritual writer, Srila Prabhupad, had spent some of his most creative years, translating and writing the commentaries on the first canto of the Shrimad Bhagavatam – considered his masterpiece by many.

Hemant had bought plenty of gorgeous twenty-two carat gold jewelry for Dafina, and a royal red sari made of the finest silk, as well as plenty of other beautiful gifts.

The three ladies in charge of preparing her for the wedding did an incredible job.

Dafina looked like a real Indian goddess.

With the crown on her head, that gorgeous red silk sari, and her impeccable make-up, she looked surreal.

Her arms and legs were decorated with beautiful artwork from henna, as is customary in Indian weddings.

After all the rituals for an auspicious marriage had been performed with the appropriate chanting of the mantras conducted by the head priest of the Krishna-Balarama temple in Vrindavan, His Grace Mukunda Datta Prabhu, there was the most delicious feast of sixty-four dishes. This dinner reception feast was cooked by the priests of Shri Shri Radha Damodar temple and served to the guests that attended the wedding ceremony.

The dinner took place in the temple courtyard.

It was beginning of March, and the evening was very pleasant.

In the serenity of that magical night, the bells from the different nearby temples could be heard ringing. Melodious songs from the evening prayers were melting the hearts of everyone assembled there.

Dafina had never tasted anything like this sanctified food in her whole life, and she had traveled to so many temples in India.

A lot of people attended the wedding and gave their blessings to the newlyweds.

Everybody admired Dafina's beauty.

When the feast was over, she went back with Hemant to the temple room.

The Temple President led them into a smaller room with beautiful pictures and statues, placed on the right side of the main altar.

Five musicians awaited them.

The custom was for the newlyweds to be serenaded throughout the whole night, till dawn.

Dafina had felt tired, but when she heard the first chords her eyes opened up in delight. The music seemed to be coming directly from the spiritual world.

She thought: "Am I dreaming, or is this really happening?"

She felt that she saw the Lord there and then in front of her.

The musicians were from all around the country. One was playing mridanga, a kind of a two-sided drum. Another was playing the harmonium, the third a sitar, and the fourth karatals— hand cymbals. The fifth one led the singing, and the others followed.

Dafina and Hemant knew some of the songs and sang along.

Not only she didn't feel exhausted, but she

even felt energized. The spiritual music infused her with an intense feeling of being overjoyed.

After dawn, they finally headed home.

Dafina made sure to take all the musicians' information, so she would be able to contact them again in the future.

After the wedding, they went on a honeymoon, travelling to the most beautiful parts of India. She visited many new holy places, but the one that made the deepest impression on her was Jagannath Puri on the Bay of Bengal in Orissa.

I'm sure she will tell you many incredible things about that special town in her stories. But it would take too much time if I were to try to repeat what I've heard from her.

In any case, when the honeymoon was over, they returned to Vrindavan.

Hemant was supposed to leave for the United States soon, and Dafina intended to stay two more months with her father-in-law before returning to Europe, where she would wait for her green card.

Hemant's brother, Pranav, who was not married, would be staying with them too.

Hemant's mother had passed away a long time ago, when he was only twelve years old and his brother seven.

From the very first encounters with her brother-in-law, Dafina felt that something was off with him, but she didn't know what.

As the time passed, some of her belongings

started to disappear.

One day, completely horrified, she'd found that about a third of her luxurious wedding jewelry was missing.

Hemant was still there at the time, and she confided in him.

They decided to report the robbery to the police station.

Dafina had never seen such sluggish police officers. They were only interested in getting their paychecks. They didn't seem eager to solve the mystery or find the thief.

After some time, Hemant was supposed to leave. He had already taken five weeks of vacation.

Her brother-in-law was not with them all the time in the house. He would come and go.

Whenever he was around, some of Dafina's belongings would mysteriously disappear - a beautiful silk sari, some of her western clothes, some money, a nice souvenir she had picked up in India during their honeymoon.

Soon it became clear who was responsible for that, and it was a great disappointment. Her brother-in-law looked so innocent. He had beautiful eyes, and Dafina loved people who had beautiful eyes.

She kept going with her father-in-law to report the robberies at the police station, but they both felt it was useless.

"We know who the thief is," her father-in-law

said one evening, "and we pretend we don't know."

Dafina kept silent.

Then her father-in-law opened his heart and shared that Pranav was mad, a sick man, and had given him so much suffering throughout his whole life. He shared that this sort of behavior had embarrassed him wherever they went. Pranav had made trouble with so many of their family members and close friends, and so they had lost touch with those parts of the family.

Dafina: "What is he sick from?"

Her father-in-law: "Paranoia."

Dafina: "Not something else?"

Her father-in-law: "It's paranoia".

But later, Hemant told her that it was severe schizophrenia.

Dafina: "Maybe he had missed motherly love. Maybe he needed more love."

At that her father-in-law got offended. He told her that he had given Pranav a lot of love, and that Pranav's character had nothing to do with him. He had done his best as a father, but Pranav had just turned out crazy because he was a bad person.

"I did my best to help him out, getting the good doctors, asking him to take his medications regularly, but Pranav never listened to me, never did what I told him."

So, he went on throughout the whole evening, hammering on about what a bad person Pranav was, and not even once mentioned anything good about him.

That's when Dafina really started feeling uneasy— not because of Pranav, as she had already forgiven him for stealing so many things from her, but because of her father-in-law.

"If this man can't find even a single good thing about his son, then what about the others? What about me in the future? I don't feel comfortable listening to him anymore."

Besides talking about Pranav, her father-in-law was always saying very bad things about Hemant's ex-wife. In a similar manner, he never said one good thing about her.

Dafina felt that she had pretty much been poisoned by listening to those talks, and when she returned to Europe, she decided to brush it off and not bother anymore.

MR. DALTON

DAFINA WROTE A LETTER TO THE PRESIDENT OF THE United States. She was honest, saying that she doesn't know anything about politics— it's neither her passion nor her strong side. In fact, she doesn't even watch the news.

What she wanted to talk about was his books, which were about his life before he became president. She has read both and wanted to express her opinions. She really liked his style and considered him a good writer.

She mentioned to him also how she is a struggling writer, originally from Southern Europe, and living now with her husband in the States.

At the end of the letter, she asked him for his blessings so that she could also make it as a writer in the US.

Dafina didn't type the letter but sent it hand-written.

Her husband teased her that she would never get a reply because of that. Who would bother nowadays with a hand-written letter, he said. Certainly not the President of the United States.

But after some time, his reply came. It was typed on a beautiful piece of paper with the memorandum of the White House.

> *"Dear Mrs. Dafina Kumar,*
>
> *Thank you for taking the time to write. I have heard many personal accounts from individuals and families across our country, and I appreciate your sharing your story with me.*
>
> *Each day, I read letters from people, so I can stay connected to their real-life and diverse experiences.*
>
> *Thank you again for sharing your story with me. I wish you all the best in the future,*
>
> *Sincerely…"*

So, why should my girlfriend talk politics with the President of the United States when she wants to talk literature?

DAFINA

Besides the other good that he is doing for me, Alec did me a huge favor that he will never know about.

Since I fell in love with him, I've completely erased from my subconscious mind a Swiss guy that I was suffering over for years and years.

We'd met at Zurich TV a long time ago, where I used to work for a couple of months.

When I first saw him, I immediately felt a very deep connection to him, like I had somehow always known him.

Sometimes you see somebody for the first time, but you have the feeling that you've known him forever. That's what happened with us.

We were both single at that time, but despite a strong physical attraction between us, we somehow never got sexual.

Most probably because we had both worked so hard - day in and day out - me as a scriptwriter and him as a director.

There were all those deadlines to be met, all those projects to be finalized. I could hardly catch my breath, nor could he.

A couple of years ago, he showed up miraculously at a glamorous party in Raleigh.

I was without my husband, as usual, surrounded by my friends like a queen with her ladies in waiting.

He was with his wife, and I was disappointed that she was not a beauty, at least not externally.

When he saw me, he couldn't believe that I was there in front of him, so we kept looking at each other for a few minutes.

I turned away and continued to have fun at the party, talking with different people, laughing.

He kept staring at me, staring the whole night, even his wife noticed and started feeling uncomfortable.

But he didn't have the guts to approach me that evening.

After that, he visited the area a couple of more times, and some of our mutual friends told me that he had been inquiring about me. He wanted to meet me and talk to me.

Somehow, I didn't feel the same way anymore.

"What for?" I thought. "Now we're both married."

Obviously, I was still being prudish.

I even asked a few of my close friends to do me a favor— if they knew that he would be coming, to warn me ahead of time, so that I wouldn't show up and run into him.

But Alec did the job. His presence in my life had erased the Swiss guy forever.

Who is going to be the man to erase Alec Dalton from my heart and mind when the time comes?

I don't even want to think about that.

SAM

It's seven something in the evening. The three of us are in my apartment, sitting up on the king bed, our backs against the headboard.

Dafina is between me and Kazuo, eating roasted vegetables with soya sauce. Kazuo and I are eating sushi.

We're watching her favorite show, "Two and a Half Men" with Charlie Sheen, and laughing like crazy.

It's hard to eat, though, because we can't stop laughing.

According to Dafina, the show is a masterpiece. An example of great television art.

She only wants to watch the episodes with Charlie Sheen. Those scripts, she says, are much better than the later ones.

"That's my professional defect, sweetie. I always focus on the story and the script the most," she tells me.

I love to see her laugh.

I love to imagine her being on the stage and getting an Oscar for best original script.

LIDIA

DAFINA HASN'T CALLED ME IN A LONG TIME.
I hope she's doing alright.

MR. DALTON

MY GIRLFRIEND KNOWS TWO THINGS FOR SURE.

She knows about God. And she knows about love.

Her body is different than other women I've been with.

It's not like a grave of slaughtered animals.

Our being together is God's arrangement, and nobody else's.

LIDIA

In the first year of her stay in the US, besides cooking at the temple regularly, Dafina was also preparing for a bunch of theatre festivals.

She'd pick some story from the scriptures that was appropriate for the occasion and make a nice script from it.

The devotees from the temple, who were enthusiastic to take part, would support her in every effort: creating nice costumes, setting up the stage, coming regularly to the rehearsals, and learning their dialogue by heart.

The audience was very happy with her work, and many people had told her that in more than twenty-five years being in the community, they'd never seen better plays.

One day she got sick, and Hemant told her he would bring her some homeopathic medicine from Whole Foods that had no side effects.

When he returned, she noticed that the bar

code was missing, and realized that Hemant had stolen the medicine.

She freaked out completely.

"How could you do that?! How could you! You better start thinking about getting out of the house and getting a real job! Pretending that you're doing something online won't help us. You're only losing money!"

She was horrified.

"Is this the man I fell in love with? When he proposed to me and married me, I thought I was the luckiest woman on Earth! Now he's a completely different person."

Hemant would reply furiously: "Don't lecture me!"

Dafina stormed out of the flat and went to a nearby pond to pacify herself. She was sitting there on a bench for hours crying, still not believing that Hemant would steal, and on the biggest festival of the Hindu year, apperence of Lord Krishna, Krishna Janmashthami.

She couldn't tolerate the poverty anymore, and in a few months, she found work as a receptionist at a beauty salon.

The owner was an Indian lady whose name was Shilpa.

Dafina was warned that Shilpa was very stingy and verbally abusive, and that she was unable to keep her employees for long because of her awful attitude.

Dafina needed money, though, so she disregarded all the warnings.

One morning it was very slow. Nobody was there, and the lady who did eyebrows decided to do it for Dafina and for the other girl who was working the same shift. Shilpa came a little later, and when she noticed what had happened, she got enraged and chastised all three of them horribly.

Dafina didn't understand what the crime was. They weren't neglecting any customers.

When she told her friends that she had gotten that job, they told her not to advertise the news, because Indians are widely known to be very unpleasant bosses.

They are very demanding, they offer very little money, and they scold and chastise you in front of everybody. They don't mind if they lash out at you. For them, that's normal. Hurt feelings? Who cares?

Shilpa was living proof of it.

For no reason, she'd yell at Dafina. Like why had she done her hair so glamorously that morning? Or why was she wearing high heels?

"You're only a receptionist. You're not on a runway or red carpet. There's no need for you to try so hard to look stunning. Whom do you want to seduce? Only ladies come here."

"First of all, I like to look good for myself," Dafina immediately replied, "because it makes me feel better. And then for everybody else."

Maybe Shilpa had noticed that her husband was giving very approving glances to Dafina whenever he'd come inside the salon.

He was some high executive at SAS, and they lived in a million-dollar home.

Dafina was working Saturdays and Sundays from morning till evening for only five dollars an hour. Monday was her only day off.

When she'd try to ask for a little better pay, Shilpa would turn a deaf ear.

"Do your job quietly and don't bother me anymore. I think I'm fair with you. If you don't like it here, I can easily find somebody else who will work even for less."

A few months passed, and Dafina realized that she'd had enough.

The money she was making was not worth her time. When she'd come home, she'd have no strength to do anything, including her writing.

After Dafina left, Shilpa hired one girl after another, three girls in all, as replacements. Each of the girls left within a week.

DAFINA

Some American guys will tell you with an attitude: "You're a knock-out. I'd like to fuck you." But that's a culture shock for me.

Here are the stories of my three American boyfriends when I was single, long before Mr. Dalton came into my life.

Bruce Maxwell, whom I met through our mutual friends in Zurich.

He was there on vacation, when I used to work at Zurich TV.

After dinner at our friend's mansion on Zuriberg Fluntern, he invited me for a walk.

The evening was very pleasant, full of stars. A light breeze was blowing, that October night. It felt good to be outside.

From Zuriberg Fluntern, which is one of the most prestigious parts of the city, to the downtown of Zurich is just fifteen minutes by foot.

So, I was happy to exercise a bit after the opulent meal.

Bruce looks like a kind and intelligent man. He's tall, blond and blue-eyed. Not exactly handsome, but pretty charming.

A guy who you can tell feels very comfortable in his skin.

He's a bit older than me. Divorced with four sons. Lives in Sarasota, Florida.

He has a Jewish background, and his father, who's in his late eighties, lives in a luxurious condo on the Avenue of Americas.

His mother had passed away a long time ago.

He has one younger brother who lives in Singapore with his wife and two children.

Our talk that evening goes pretty smooth.

I'm impressed how much he knows about Europe. Obviously, he likes to travel, and uses every opportunity to do so.

He tells me casually that when he becomes super rich, he'll move to Europe for good.

"All the richest Americans are crazy for Europe. They feel good here."

So, we share our memories about our favorite places like Paris and Venice, Vienna and Copenhagen, Budapest and Saint Petersburg, Athens and Istanbul.

He mentions the islands Malta and Sicily, Santorini and Salamina, and I can't believe that he's visited them all and knows their history too.

The guy is obviously very smart and well-informed.

So, we're walking and talking in that pleasant night when I tell him that I feel tired and would like to go to my hotel. He proposes to accompany me, which I appreciate.

From that evening on, we meet every day for coffee and lunch, dinners and movies.

He's very respectful and never tries anything, which is a pleasant surprise for me. He takes his time getting to know me better.

This is really a relief, especially after the debacle with the Swiss guy from the TV industry, who was so hot for me but proved to be too hesitant and clumsy to even try to play one derby with me.

Bruce always pays for everything, doesn't even let me reach for my wallet at all.

I'm smart enough to realize that, compared to him, (as we say in Macedonia) I'm poor as a church mouse.

It's not hard to tell that he's extremely comfortable with money.

After a couple of weeks, he's supposed to fly back to Sarasota, and we exchange phone numbers and e-mails.

The communication continues, I'm still working in Zurich and he's already making plans for me to visit him.

I must finish my contract assignment in Zurich first, and when I return to Macedonia, I must ask for permission to take my month of paid vacation.

Bruce pays for my return ticket and sends me two thousand dollars, so I can buy things that I might need.

He welcomes me at the Sarasota Airport with a big bouquet of flowers and helps me with my luggage.

He picks me up in his black BMW SUV.

On the way to his home, we're laughing and joking, and he tells me that I look surprisingly fresh after such a long trip. Little does he know, I've changed three flights.

He tells me that I'm beautiful.

When we reach his neighborhood, I'm kind of dumbstruck. There are huge mansions all around.

It's just one week before Christmas, and everything is stunningly decorated.

He goes to his driveway, and I see that his home is a grandiose, beautiful mansion, Spanish style, saffron terracotta color, with a lot of pillars, small and big balconies, and beautifully designed windows.

The whole building is illuminated with different color lights. It looks like a palace from the Disney movies.

I try hard not to show how impressed I am.

He leads me to my room, which is enormous, with a beautiful bathroom.

Everything looks clean and perfect.

He tells me that he has a housekeeper who visits every day, works five to six hours and then goes home.

The two of his eldest sons live in separate houses that he already bought for them, and the two younger ones live with him, but spend more time at their girlfriends' houses than at home.

He tells me for the first time that his sons are dark-skinned, because his ex-wife is a black lady from South America.

He seems to expect me to judge him, but I see nothing unusual about that. I've never been a racist, because that's not the way how I was raised.

That first night he leaves me alone. I'm very tired and I sleep well.

The next morning, I tell him that I can cook for him, and the housekeeper can take care of the cleaning.

He agrees, despite not believing that I can be trusted with cooking.

"You're a writer. How come you can cook? In the United States, lady writers are usually very proud that they can't, and don't like to cook."

"My mother didn't like to cook, so I was obliged to learn cooking from a very early age, if I wanted to have decent meals. By the time I was fourteen, I'd already learned how to cook pretty much everything."

He was amazed.

Then, the next day, Bruce starts acting like he doesn't have any time for me.

He works in the office of his home. He's very

busy all the time and only communicates with me when we take our meals and when we have sex.

The rest of the day, he's absent.

He praises my cooking and praises my love making.

Other than that, he gives me the attitude that I'm nothing special, and that he needs somebody who is really special.

His vibe is that he's too good for me.

On the second day of my stay, he starts complaining about his mother, that she was a bad woman and a horrible mother.

"She never told me that she loves me. She would beat me and humiliate me in front of my friends."

And he started crying in front of me like a child.

In those moments, I felt very sorry for him.

He cried and cried and couldn't stop crying for a long time. I tried giving him a hug, but he pushed me away.

"Leave me alone," he said. "I don't need your compassion. Who are you to give me solace? You're just a whore. You were dumbstruck when you saw who I am, what I've achieved. You think I'm stupid, that I didn't notice your admiration. You thought I wasn't going to notice. You thought I was stupid. But I'm not stupid. You're stupid. You think you can conquer my heart. Well, you're wrong.

If I fuck you, it doesn't mean I love you. I've never loved any woman. I hate them all.

And I fuck you good. Don't I fuck you good?

Am I good enough for you?

Tell me. Tell me, you European whore.

You're religious, you say, but I never saw anybody in my life who enjoys sex as much as you do. And I've had a lot of women. But you're the number one whore, I can tell. The one who gives the most pleasure."

I wanted to escape, to run away, but he kept holding me tight with his big hands.

This tantrum has happened on the second night after my arrival, after we made love for the first time.

My return ticket was a month later. How was I going to survive in this huge mansion with this crazy man?

The days of my stay were pretty much like that.

Bruce's moods changed a hundred times a day.

I found out that he was making his money through online trading, and that he was pretty good at it. He worked on the computer all day with his legs up on the table.

He would toot his own horn all the time and tell people that he made a couple of million dollars a year.

I believed it too.

He never graduated from college. He had flunked chemistry his sophomore year and that was it.

He made it very clear that my duties were to cook for him, because he liked it a lot, and to give him sex, because he loved it, whenever he wanted.

He made it very clear that I was nothing more than an extraordinary whore who just happened to be a great cook.

I did my best to be obedient and not talk back.

In between, sometimes we would go to the beach.

One day he forgot the chairs that we had brought along with us.

Instead of going back and getting them from his home, he just went to a store nearby and bought a new set.

Spending money was easy for him. He never thought twice about it.

I'd never met a guy like that before.

In the meantime, he badmouthed all the women in his life, starting with his ex-wife, who he described as a demon, a devil from hell, and going through all of his previous girlfriends.

He's never told me a single good thing about any of them.

Of course, he never forgot to remind me how much he hated his mother, and how he hoped she was burning in hell.

I was terribly scared by this man. Horrified.

I never enjoyed the sex with him after that first time.

I did it whenever he requested, because I was scared that something worse might happen if I refused.

I couldn't escape.

I had no car. I didn't know the place. I had no friends. I didn't know anybody there.

I didn't even have access to the Internet.

That whole month, I never saw anybody walking on the streets of that luxurious neighborhood.

I tried to be invisible, not to irritate him, staying in my room and just reading books.

I prayed to God that I could somehow just go home sooner.

When he was in a good mood, he would shower me with the most wonderful words and lavish me with gifts.

Every few days, he would give me a thousand dollars and drop me off in some fancy store.

He would pay for luxurious spa treatments, massages, hair styling, the dentist.

He felt happy when I spent a lot of money and bought lots of things. He'd encourage me to spend more.

"I will give you much more money if you want. Don't be shy. You're a very good person, and I love you very much. I think you're very special. I'll spend thousands of dollars on you if you love me in return, as I do."

I really couldn't understand how he could become so affectionate so suddenly.

I got the weird feeling that two different souls were living in his body at the same time.

"I'm not a bad man, Dafina. Please don't leave me. Please, stay with me. If you leave me, I'll hate myself eternally. I'll feel like a complete failure."

"Please, Dafina, don't be mad at me. I love you. You are gorgeous, you're special, you're such a beautiful woman. And a beautiful person, too. Stay with me, and I will give you whatever you want."

At that time, I didn't know much about mental illnesses. Looking back, I can see now that he probably had a severe bipolar disorder, with all the signs of manic depression.

In his eyes, you could see that he wasn't all there.

For my birthday, he got me a fifteen-thousand-dollar golden watch, which Mr. Dalton certainly has noticed. I still wear it on my right wrist.

It costs much more than our two Lincoln Town Cars together.

Maybe you don't think I really know how much it cost, but he paid for it right in front of me.

What actually happened was that I had lost my cheap watch on the beach a day before, and Bruce wanted to make me happy by buying me a new one.

We were walking on the streets in Sarasota when we stopped in front of a high-end jewelry store. Next to the jewelry, a long row of magnificent watches was placed in the window.

When we entered the store, the salesman greeted us not just politely but almost submissively.

Bruce told him that we were interested in women's watches.

The salesman opened a drawer and took out a tray with some gorgeous watches on it.

After some time, I picked up the one I liked the best.

Bruce takes it is his hand.

He smiles at me: "You like this watch?"

"Yes."

"It's yours."

Without blinking, he swipes his credit card and I have the watch on my wrist.

In his car, he tells me that he loves me to death.

"You're a golden girl. You deserve a golden watch. It really suits your personality perfectly. You're my perfect girl. I never met anyone as smart and sweet as you. And I'm a smart guy. My IQ is 150."

"You're making me a better person, too. That's for sure. With you, I feel like I can be a better person. I can improve. I can thrive. Don't leave me please. I can extend your ticket. That's not a problem for me to pay a couple of hundred more. Think about it. You can leave your job. I have money to support you. You're going to feel like a queen."

So, besides enduring the manic tantrums that happened every few evenings with all the horrible insults, I was also witnessing more of his tender and vulnerable side. He'd tell me he loved me more than he'd ever loved any woman, that I'm the one he wants to spend his life with.

His three elder sons had accepted me wonderfully. They thought I was very cool. Only the youngest one was grumpy and refused to talk to me.

His ex-wife was living with her new husband in Miami, and she never visited her sons.

That year, she just sent them a Christmas card.

I felt very relieved when the month was over.

As soon as I got back home, he kept calling and e-mailing me to come back, and I was polite enough to still talk to him for a while, but one day I had enough and couldn't pretend anymore.

I humbly asked him never to call me or write me again.

I told him, "You're a great man, but I don't think we can be a couple."

My second American boyfriend was also from Florida, from Fort Lauderdale.

We met online.

His name was Tom Mancini, an Italian American, and a stunningly good-looking man.

You could really lose yourself in his beautiful brown eyes.

When he saw my pictures, he booked his ticket immediately for two weeks in Macedonia.

He was rich too, but not even close to Bruce Maxwell.

He had a big beautiful house and three fancy cars, which he made sure to show me online, so I could see that he was well to do.

He was divorced and had one son who was living with his ex-wife somewhere in Pennsylvania.

I waited for him at the airport, and when he saw me he grinned from ear to ear.

"It's so good to see you, Dafina! I couldn't wait."

I brought him to the Holiday Inn in downtown Skopje.

We went to the front desk to book his room.

In our correspondence, I had made it clear that he couldn't stay in my apartment, that I respect his privacy and need my own. That way, we'd both feel more comfortable.

It wasn't an issue for him, because he has a lot of cash.

So, we were in the elevator going up to his room.

We entered, and he was very pleased with the view. He said how Skopje was a beautiful place, and how happy he was to be here.

Without even washing his face or brushing his teeth after such a long trip, he just unzips his pants and pulls down his underwear.

I was completely horrified.

I was thinking: "Is this possible?"

I was totally appalled and couldn't hide it.

Seeing my discomfort, he frowned.

"What's the matter? Why are you so nervous? Have you not seen a naked man before?"

I kept quiet. I was just left without words.

He yelled: "I can't believe that you are not ready for me. I flew all the way from the other part of the world to be with you, and you're not ready for me? Goddamnit, I don't get it. What's wrong with you? Are you fucking kidding me?"

I tried to apologize, and mumbled something under my breath…

"You don't like me?"

"I do, but…"

"But what? If you like me, why should we waste our time? I'm only here for two weeks, remember? I can't stay forever."

I didn't know what to say. I was just terribly disappointed.

He became so bitter, that he started finding fault with everything. Not in me, but in everything else— how everything was so expensive in Macedonia, how the mattress wasn't soft enough, how the hotel staff wasn't very kind to him, how they served only five kinds of cheeses for breakfast…

Fortunately, he got so deeply offended by my initial rejection that he never approached me again, and so we never had sex— which was a great relief.

I didn't like his energy, after all.

Still, he was gentleman enough to take me on a nice trip to Istanbul for five days. I've been there twice before and had recommended it to him when he'd asked me which places were worth visiting.

He paid for everything: the airplane tickets, the hotel, all the excursions. He got me plenty of nice gifts too.

He was very grateful that I had told him about this terrific place.

In due course of time, he warmed up to me, and told me that he liked me as a dear friend, that he wasn't angry with me anymore for not getting sexual. Basically, that he understood.

He even apologized for scaring me.

"It dawned on me that European girls are different. That you have a different culture."

"It's all okay," I said.

I tried to be nice and charming, but not overly seductive so he wouldn't jump on me again. I tried to play it cool, to be understanding, to smile all the time, to be bubbly, and to tell him interesting stories.

As I went on, he became so enthralled that he wanted to tell me his story too.

When he was eighteen, he went to fight in Vietnam.

"I killed a lot of people there."

"Did you?"

"Yes. Many."

He said that with an attitude like he was talking about ants.

"Till today I can never sleep peacefully. I always sleep with one eye open. In fact, I sleep with my gun next to me."

I was like "O.K."

So, then he told me that when he was in high school, he set a factory on fire near his house.

The whole factory burned down, and they never caught him.

He told me that he has never hit a woman, but if his ex-wife came his way he'd beat her horribly, with his fists, with his legs, with whatever....

"Why do you hate her so much?"

"My son took his stepfather's last name. That's what she did to me. She didn't let him keep my name."

Tom was usually pretty kind to me, but I still felt uneasy around him, and couldn't wait for his visit to end.

I was sure that I didn't want to stay in touch with him.

Deep down, I felt there was something very weird about him that made me very uncomfortable.

He finally left.

And after some time, a few of my friends asked me about him.

I lied to them: "I got the news that he was killed in a bike accident."

"That's so sad. He looked like a nice man."

"He was," I replied.

"God rest his soul."

My third American boyfriend is described in my book "East Boston Blues".

He was definitely a character.

MR. DALTON

LIFE IS GOOD.

It's what you make out of it.

How you shape it.

My life is good, because Dafina is part of it.

I believe in karma. We've recognized each other from another life.

DAFINA

I'M STILL HELPING MY HUSBAND IN HIS BUSINESS, AND most of the time I'm driving men around.

One morning, I'm supposed to pick up a gentleman from Clayton and bring him to the airport. I'm there ahead of time, and he's already waiting for me in the driveway.

I get out from the car to be polite and greet him.

He's an elderly gentleman in his sixties, grey haired with blue eyes, impeccably dressed in a designer suit, thousand-dollar shoes and a Louis Vuitton suitcase.

I'm kind of impressed, maybe my most glamorous customer so far.

"Good morning, sir."

When he sees me, he starts laughing, amazed?

"You're my ride? Ha, ha, ha…You must be kidding me."

I start laughing too, because his laughter is just

so contagious and jolly.

So, we're both laughing like crazy, in front of his mansion very early in the morning.

To be honest, I don't get it but I'm laughing because it feels good and it's nice to see him laugh.

After some time, he finally stops.

"Pretty lady, you're good company, but if you don't mind, I'll be your chauffeur this time."

"Oh…All right."

So, he puts his luggage in the trunk, which I close, and climbs into the driver's seat.

I sit in the back and we start our trip to the airport.

So many men would love to hear my story but, by God's mercy, I somehow lure them into telling me theirs.

I don't like to tell my stories for free. They're too valuable to me.

I like to hear stories. That's what keeps me doing this job.

I'm thinking how to get this classy gentleman to tell me his stories, how to probe him without seeming aggressive, but I feel sleepy.

He asks where I'm from, a usual question. Men always tell me they love my accent.

I say: "Southern Europe, Macedonia…"

"Wow, that's cool," says the gentleman.

He is driving and looking at me through the mirror, and I'm closing my eyes.

In an instant, I fall asleep.

Next thing I know, we're at the airport, and he's gently shaking my shoulder, trying to wake me up.

"Oh, I'm so sorry, sir. Last night, I only slept a few hours."

"I understand. You must have been very busy."

I know where he's coming from, but I ignore it.

"How much do I owe you?"

"It's all right, sir. Why should you pay? You did the job."

"I don't play like this. How much is the rate?"

"With a discount, it's hundred dollars."

He gets slightly irritated: "Don't bother with the discount, please."

He gives me a hundred and fifty, and softly touches my face.

"You're beautiful, you know. Take good care of yourself."

"Thank you, sir. Have a safe flight."

I personally think highly of men. They can be so smart and strong, but sometimes they can really surprise me in a very negative way.

Most of our customers, as I've already mentioned, are CEOs and high-ranking executives.

So, why can't they keep their mouths shut in front of my husband, and talk all the time so nicely about me. Is it so difficult to be discreet?

I expect a little more brains from them, but instead they just glorify me openly in front of Hemant, what a gorgeous woman I am, what a great provider.

And it's so ridiculous. Some of them can't hide their disappointment when they see my husband picking them up instead of me, as they had hoped.

One time a gentleman gives me his credit card, so I can write the slip, but when I check in my purse I realize I've forgotten my glasses at home. I can't read without them.

So, I humbly ask the gentleman if he doesn't mind lending me his glasses.

He smiles and hands me his glasses.

I write the receipt, and he gives me a huge tip.

SAM

Kazuo is away in Hong Kong on business. Now I can spend some time with Dafina.

She cooks every day and invites me over for lunch and dinner.

I love her cooking.

Her husband is a great cook too, but he rarely cooks. He's always crazy busy.

After our meals, we usually go to the movies.

Dafina always takes her own car, because she doesn't want her husband to know that I'm going with her.

He is not accepting of gay people.

With Dafina's Regal Card, we can sometimes get free popcorn and soft drinks, prerelease screenings and movie tickets, because she has a lot of points.

Today, something terrific happened to me.

I got a card from my son and my daughter.

The card was beautiful, and they wrote: "We

love you, dad."

I showed it to Dafina.

"I told you they were going to come around."

It really means a lot to me.

DAFINA

Wʜᴇɴ I ꜱᴀᴡ Mʀ. Dᴀʟᴛᴏɴ ꜰᴏʀ ᴛʜᴇ ꜰɪʀꜱᴛ ᴛɪᴍᴇ, I thought: "Good-looking man."

But that doesn't really mean much to me. Almost nothing.

Until a man opens his mouth, I can't tell if I like him or not. Even more important for me is whether he's good at heart.

Somehow, I immediately liked Mr. Dalton's energy.

From that first encounter, I felt a deep connection. Like he might be somebody I used to know many lifetimes ago, someone who was very close and dear to me.

From the start, I felt very comfortable with him.

I felt that nothing unpleasant could happen to me.

I felt safe.

I got the impression that he was a sweet, refined and intelligent man.

Clearly, I couldn't miss that he is hardworking and pretty focused too, and I admire those qualities in a man.

Especially when they're successful but stay humble, I respect them even more.

From day one, our conversation was very smooth.

He's never tried to tell me how to drive, like some other men.

He never scolded me for speeding, and I do speed a lot.

Some gentlemen complain behind my back to my husband that I'm speeding, and to tell you the truth I find them disgusting.

LIDIA

THE FIRST YEAR OF HER STAY IN CARY, DAFINA TOLD ME that they were struggling financially the most.

Different creditors would call a hundred times a day, literally a hundred.

It was like in the horror movies, when somebody is chasing you day in and day out and you just can't escape.

Hemant would answer the phone: "Hemant Kumar is not here."

Besides her regular daily prayers, Dafina started finding solace in reading good books and listening to classical music, operas, and Spanish guitar.

One time she was listening to Beethoven when she heard somebody knocking very aggressively on the front door.

When Dafina got up and opened it, an elderly lady with thick glasses was there with a huge envelope.

Dafina apologized: "I'm sorry, I didn't hear

you. The music was very loud."

"Yes, I could hear it, and I knew somebody had to be home."

It was a creditor complaining about the missing payments, saying that if Hemant doesn't pay soon he could end up in jail.

So many times, Dafina got that warning over the phone.

"Tell your husband he can end up in jail."

Dafina is strong, very strong. But she's not a stone.

And she's pregnant.

Finally, they just shut off their home phone.

DAFINA

Wʜᴇɴ I ᴜꜱᴇᴅ ᴛᴏ ᴡᴏʀᴋ ɪɴ ᴛʜᴇ TV ɪɴᴅᴜꜱᴛʀʏ, ᴛʜᴇʀᴇ were many good bosses, for whom I had a lot of respect, and I was happy to follow their instructions.

Of course, a few were real jerks and I had trouble cooperating with them, because I didn't find them qualified enough to tell me how to do my job.

By the way, I never wanted to become a boss myself, even when I was offered the position, because I don't think I have gift for that.

I'm not good at managing people, and I've never had an interest in it.

The creative part of the job is what has always given me the most pleasure.

That's my strongest side, something I love to do the most and know how to do the best: writing original scripts, or adapting books into scripts, or correcting and improving other writers' scripts.

Nowadays, that's the writing of my novels and

short stories.

It's the most precious thing to me.

It puts me in a state of mind to completely forget about reality and enter a beautiful world, a different world, the best cure for my soul.

One boss that I got along with very well was my cousin Bobby.

When he became head of our department, it didn't do much to elevate my position there, because I already had my name.

I don't think many people knew we were cousins. We were very discreet about that.

Bobby is ten years older than me and stunningly attractive.

He's smart, rich and very talented. He had directed some of the best TV movies in the history of our broadcasting company, but in the last few years he had abandoned his artistic ambitions and became an owner of an exclusive and very expensive hotel that only hosts customers from the foreign embassies and consulates in Skopje.

He's shrewd and capable of making even more money than he did as a director. Knowing well the economic circumstances in Macedonia, I perfectly understand my cousin's intentions.

So, I was the one who was supposed to work very hard, and to be the central pillar of our department, so I could back him up and he could spend more time managing his hotel.

That arrangement worked out perfectly for

both of us.

He gave me the freedom to choose which projects I wanted to do, and to visit the most prestigious TV festivals throughout Europe.

Besides being first cousins and colleagues, we are also soulmates and very good friends.

We would often go get drinks and dinner together. Many people who didn't know that we're related assumed that I'm his newest mistress.

In public, we look like a very good couple.

Being a ladies man all his life, Bobby is smart enough to never hit on me though.

And he's full of incredible stories about his adventures.

I'm a very good listener, and I have lots of fun with him.

Also, he knows that he can count on me any time to cover for him in front of his wife.

I gave him permission to tell her that he was out with me when he was with some of his conquests.

Still, it's hard for me to understand why he feels a need to be with so many other women.

His wife is beautiful, a college professor in the medical field, and from a rich family. They have two beautiful sons.

He reminds me of my girlfriend, Lidia, whom I love deeply too.

But they're both so different than me.

I try not to judge them and, even more difficult, not to resent them.

I'm very close with Bobby, and I have guts to ask him: "Why, Bobby? Why do you need to be with other women?"

He just looks at me with his beautiful eyes and says: "Because something's missing, Dafina. Something is missing. And it's very difficult to explain that. Honestly, I don't think you can get me, until you are in the same position, when everything from outside looks so perfect about your marriage, and still you feel lonely. So incredibly lonely."

I look at him. He's right, I don't get him. I don't know what he's talking about.

I just ask him humbly: "Can you get me another drink, please?"

"Sure, I can."

"Thank you."

SAM

———

Since she moved to the States, Dafina had attracted a lot of people into her life. Some are still around, and some have left.

Dafina is very social and likes people. Because Hemant is never around, she made a schedule for the week so that somebody is visiting for dinner or drinks every evening. Dafina likes to cook and entertain.

She told me that the apartment where she grew up in downtown Skopje was like a train station, people always coming and going.

Her parents loved having people around.

They also liked having quiet time for themselves. So, there was a nice balance.

Her average week looks something like this:

Mondays: Peggy and Jimmy.

Tuesdays: Me and Kazuo (if he's in town; if not, then just me, but I'm pretty much always with her anyways).

Wednesdays: Karen and Robert.

Thursdays: Lucrecia and David.

Fridays: Eric and Melinda (when they're together, but usually they're not, so someone else visits, or Dafina just has some time to herself.

Saturdays: She's at the movies all day, or in the Museum of Art, or at the Catholic Church with Ms. Yvonne for evening mass.

Sundays: She goes to the temple in Hillsborough (usually cooking, associating with devotees, or attending the program).

Peggy and Jimmy moved to Massachusetts after their son got diagnosed with autism.

Karen and Robert moved to Florida. They had some difficulties in their marriage, so Karen moved there first, and then Robert joined her after four months. It looked like they had made up, but then just the other day Karen complained to Dafina that she's been having a lot of trouble with Robert.

Why doesn't she leave him?

Because of their children. She doesn't want to be a single mother.

Also, a few of Dafina's very close friends moved out of the country for good.

Adriana got married in Lima, Peru.

Gia moved back to London, (Mr. Dalton's birthplace and his parents' hometown.)

Dafina's dearest friend from the temple community, Prema Manjari, moved to the Miami temple. When she told Dafina that she'd be moving and probably not coming back, Dafina felt a physical pain. She couldn't eat for two days and cried all the time.

Still Prema honored her, after leaving the Hillsborough temple, by spending two days in Dafina's flat and then departing to Florida from there.

They had a great time together, getting up at three in the morning, taking showers, and doing all their prayers at one time, singing the spiritual songs, and reading from the Srimad Bhagavatam.

For Dafina, it struck her as weird that someone who visited once a week for dinner, never called her back after moving out of town.

Like Peggy and Jimmy: no phone calls, no e-mails.

But if someone doesn't miss her, she certainly doesn't miss them either.

If she wants to keep them with her, she puts them in her stories. That way, they stay with her while at the same time she lets go of them forever.

Whenever her friends inquire about Hemant – where he is, why he's always absent, why he's always working – and give her sarcastic looks as if to ask what kind of husband you got – Dafina simply says he's busy, he's driving, and that's the nature of his job.

"I found my peace. I'm not suffering anymore like before."

Most of her friends, who think that they know

everything about her, because Dafina is so bubbly and entertaining all the time, have no idea that she has Mr. Dalton in her life.

Deep down she is very reclusive. A very private person.

She doesn't take it personally now when Hemant comes home angry and caustic. She knows he's not a bad person. In the last five years, his life has simply become unbalanced – all work and no fun, and he's always exhausted. So, she just brushes it off.

But before she fell for Alec, her husband used to make her cry so often, lashing out for no reason, and venting all the frustrations of his hectic schedule on her.

For a long time, she felt like a trash compactor the way he treated her.

But having her beautiful lover by her side, Dafina became not just happier and stronger but also much thicker-skinned too.

DAFINA

I NEVER USED TO CHASE MEN. THERE WAS NO NEED. They chased me, and I would choose or refuse.

I never used to hit on men. That's not who I am. That's not my way.

In my system of values, the woman should be prey and the man should be a hunter.

The other way around is just ridiculous.

A year after our first meeting, Mr. Dalton started hitting on me mildly, but in a very sophisticated, almost shy way.

In the beginning, I was reserved.

But when I was sure that he liked me, and when I had admitted to myself that I liked him too, then I allowed myself to send him a hint.

I realized it was hypocritical to behave like a stone when, deep down, I was anything but indifferent.

So, one beautiful morning when I was giving him a ride to the airport, I talked to him like this:

"You are working very hard, Sir. You have a responsible job. You have a family to take care of. Do you have any time for yourself?"

He thought for a moment, and said with some melancholy:

"Time for myself? It's hard to find. No matter what you do, it's hard... Maybe mowing the lawn. Because it's different, it relaxes my mind."

"For me, relaxing is to wash the dishes by hand. That's how I let my mind take it easy."

"That's nice, because you get two things done at once – you relax, and the dishes get clean," he replied approvingly.

I don't think I've ever heard a sexier reply from a man.

I could imagine Mr. Dalton sweating, his attractive hands gripping that lawnmower...

I just wondered, *how much strength would be left after mowing that big lawn around his beautiful house, for performing on top of me?*

LIDIA

AFTER THE MISCARRIAGE, DAFINA FOUND A PART-TIME job as an assistant teacher in a nearby preschool.

She still didn't feel physically fit but needed to work so she could pay her hospital bills.

She didn't have health insurance back then and doesn't have it now.

She was in the hospital for just four hours, but the bills were astronomical.

Being around children did her good. They immediately fell in love with her, as did their parents, and the lady principal.

In fact, the principal praised Dafina in front of the parents for how many languages she speaks, and how wonderful she is with the kids.

Shortly after Dafina's arrival, the principal started cutting hours from the other teachers and giving Dafina more hours. So, Dafina was practically working full-time.

Other teachers were going home with a smaller

paycheck, while Dafina was getting a bigger one.

That lasted a few months, but eventually the other teachers wouldn't tolerate it.

They complained about the strategy of the principal to the higher authorities, so both the lady principal and Dafina got fired.

DAFINA

I'M TRYING ON A FEW LACY BLOUSES IN FRONT OF THE mirror without a bra.

I'm thinking: "Should I show up like this in front of Mr. Dalton?"

We aren't lovers. We're just friends.

He's refined and composed, but he's a healthy man after all.

I don't want to get raped in the car.

I better behave.

SAM

Two years after losing his job, Hemant started driving the taxi.

His attempts to make money from trading on-line didn't prove lucrative. Apparently, not everyone can be Bruce Maxwell.

So, when they didn't have money for the rent, they were obliged to invite one of their bachelor friends to move in with them, and that was when Hemant finally realized he should take some other course of action.

A few times he went on interviews to get back into the field, but nothing panned out.

False accusations from his ex about failing to pay child support were getting in the way.

Some of his friends advised him to get confirmation from a lawyer that the accusations were false, that the whole issue was still under litigation.

But he never provided such a document before going for the interview, so he never got the job in the end.

One of his best friends scolded him softly: "You've been sleeping for two years when you could go in a hundred different directions to find a job."

With his taxi driving, their financial situation improved drastically, and money started to flow, so Hemant hoped to get rid of his debts slowly, but he's never home.

Dafina waited almost a year for him to invite her to the movies.

When he didn't, she just went alone.

She's always the one to suggest a date, and he's always turning her down.

He tells her in an enraged voice, yelling, so the whole building can hear: "I'm tired! TIRED. Do you understand English? TIRED. I can't move even one step to go out and have fun, after all day being outside."

So, every attempt to have some quality time together leads to a fight.

Somehow, requesting what was reasonable for a married couple made Dafina look like a very demanding wife.

He'd often fire back that she was not contributing enough, not taking responsibility, not brave enough to venture out of her comfort zone.

"You just read books, one after another. Look at yourself first, before pointing fingers at me."

When he yells at her like that, Dafina feels like

there is a horrible stranger in front of her, not her beloved husband.

"Oh, my God… is this the man who promised in front of my parents, my sister, my brother-in-law, my nephew and my niece, that he'd take wonderful care of me, even if he had to work two jobs at a time, until I could get on my feet and find my way? So I wouldn't be obliged to work out of the household, and could focus on being a wife and mother, on my writing and pushing my career?"

Dafina doesn't like to fight. She witnessed another kind of atmosphere in her home in Skopje.

She jokes that she never got dumped by a man, but her husband keeps dumping her, again and again.

She tells him: "You're always making me feel like a crap."

In the meantime, false accusations had been piling up, but he didn't do anything to fix them.

A few of his friends, and Dafina too, advised him to get a good lawyer.

"The false accusations are like a snowball rolling downhill, getting bigger and bigger. Get a lawyer and start cleaning up your mess," Dafina tells him.

"Lawyers in this country are expensive. They'll rip me off."

"That's like having cancer and not wanting to see a doctor, because he'll rip you off. But cancer can kill you, like these false accusations."

I've never met a man who was so generous in a divorce settlement as Hemant. He's just left everything to his ex, not even trying to take care of himself a little better.

For somebody who was already planning to get remarried, that attitude is just weird.

Even his lawyer in Texas told him, right to his face: "You're stupid. Nobody gives more than fifty percent, not even men much richer than you."

Instead of getting a thank you and a friendly attitude, he only got false accusations from his ex, that he wasn't paying the child support regularly.

The truth is that, on her request, he started sending the money directly to her, because she had complained that the checks from the child support agency were coming too slowly, so she couldn't pay the mortgage on time for the house that she won in the divorce.

She promised to report the payments to the child support agency but never did.

Dafina helped him get photocopies of all the checks from the bank that he had sent his ex over the years.

Her signature was on them too.

Still, his ex denied receiving any of that money.

When he asked to settle things between them, because he isn't enough of a fool to pay again what he already paid, his ex would reply: "Don't bother me. Deal with the child support agency."

Time passed, and Hemant did nothing.

He even refused to go to the agency to file the motion that he had lost his job, which had happened more than two years ago. So, they kept chasing him to pay the same amount, even though now he makes much less money than before.

Dafina begged him to get a lawyer. "You can't deal with this alone. You need help!"

Hemant turned a deaf ear.

"Once you start paying lawyers, it never ends."

"But we don't have a choice. In Macedonia, we say, 'Pay more, it will come back to you cheaper. Trying to save a couple of hundred dollars, you can lose thousands. '"

Dafina even threatened to leave him if he didn't start fixing the mess, but her words had no effect.

DAFINA

My FIRST LINE FOR GENTLEMEN, WHEN THEY SIT IN MY car is: "What time is your flight, sir?"

If I find them interesting, I try to start a conversation, so I can hear their story.

If nothing provokes me to inquire about them, I keep quiet and maintain a distant and serious attitude.

So, even if they want to talk to me, they can get the vibe that I'm not in the mood to pay extra attention to them, except to provide good service.

When we approach the airport, another line is: "Which airline are you flying, sir?"

For the ladies, my line is that they look pretty, even if they don't.

The second line is that I love them very much.

When the men fly out of town, I think: "Go ahead, guys. Fix the problems. Save the world."

When the ladies depart, I don't think anything.

MR. DALTON

My relationship with Dafina is not merely passionate, not just an explosion of sensuality, that kind of stuff.

Also, I don't see it as a game of bursting hormones between two middle-aged people.

It's much much deeper, and I'm unable to explain how or why.

She is certainly a person I'd like to spend my vacation in heaven with, but that wouldn't be enough for me.

When I pass away, and when she passes away, I'd like our souls to be together forever.

As long as we're on this earth, though, I must admit that it's not enough for me to meet her just once a month.

I want her more.

But she clearly likes to keep me yearning. And there's nothing I can do about that.

SAM

My dearest friend is coming around nine o'clock tonight to tell me some great news.

She just had her first encounter in the hotel with a man whom she loves like she's never loved any man before.

Kazuo will be here, but she doesn't mind talking in front of him.

She knows what she tells us stays within these walls.

I can't wait to hear the story.

Here comes Kazuo. He looks fresh already, despite flying into town this morning from Hong Kong.

Dafina picked him up, and he says they laughed like crazy in the car.

She was so excited that she was going to meet Alec in private that she couldn't stop talking about it. She was like a young girl on her first date, asking Kazuo to wish her luck. She confided in him that she was a little scared too.

By the way there is great news for me and Kazuo.

His wife, Aiko, has been pressing him over the last year, day after day, to sell the mansion on Giovanni Court and buy a new one in Shanghai. Kazuo decided that's not a bad idea.

He will shift her and their two daughters over there, so we can breathe more easily. That way, she can be nearer to their two sons in Tokyo.

Aiko is not a stupid woman and knows that Kazuo has somebody.

She doesn't mind though, and I admire her for that.

She believes in reincarnation and all that and is totally convinced that Kazuo and she were brother and sister in a previous life.

Much before I came into the picture, Kazuo told me that she felt that way.

When Dafina finally arrives, she is glowing.

She looks blissful, like somebody who just came down from heaven.

"Sweetie, I'm impatient. How was it?"

"Great!"

"C'mon, start with the details!"

"Oh, I don't even know where to start. We had such a wonderful time, but it went so fast. When the time came to part, I felt like crying. Oh, I've never felt happier, and now I feel like I'm flying, like I'm floating one foot off the ground."

"I can tell."

Dafina gives me a hug and kiss on the cheek, then goes to Kazuo and gives him the same.

She sits on the futon.

"Oh, let me get myself together. It was surreal. I couldn't believe it was happening."

"I understand. You need a little time. But, just tell us briefly, how he performed?"

Dafina smiles at me shyly.

"Oh Sam, look at you. No, it's not what you think. We didn't have sex."

"You didn't? Then what did you do in the hotel room?"

"We talked, we laughed. Held hands. We just enjoyed being together for the first time outside of my car."

"But, why the delay? Haven't you been dreaming about this for months already?"

"That's true. I've been dreaming, and I'm happy it finally happened."

"Then, what went wrong?"

"Nothing! It was perfect."

"But you just said that you didn't have sex?"

"Why should we? I need time to adjust, and Alec is not an aggressive man. He's refined. He saw I wasn't ready."

"Oh, my! Looks like Mother Theresa got a lover!"

"Don't make drama out of nothing, Sam."

I turn to Kazuo for help, but he's very shrewd

and doesn't show any emotions, he just has that half-smile on his mesmerizing face.

"Dafina, you've messed up!"

"I just need a little more time."

"How much more time do you need?"

"I don't know. But I know that sex will come spontaneously, at the right time. Even if it doesn't happen, I'm alright with that too. I will be happy to meet with him and talk to him. He is so supportive of me, all my dreams. He wants to see me make my living from my writing, not from driving men around."

"But you said you've known each other for a year and a half?"

"Yes, we have. So?"

"That's not enough time for you?'

"Oh, Sam. You're my best friend, but you talk to me like you don't know me at all. I understand you're worried, because you know how much Alec means to me. But everything was fine. We had great time, believe me. He enjoyed my company. He was happy and relaxed, and he was in the best mood. I told him interesting stories, and he liked them all."

'What kind of stories?"

"One of the many, I told him about Marie Antoinette, the last French queen. She's my role model for so many things. Such a great woman, but they hated her in France because she was Austrian. I'd like to make a musical about her…"

"Look Dafina, I don't know much about Southern Europe. I've never been there, and I don't know the culture. Of course, I hope to go one day and visit where you're from. But I know that when a man pays for a hotel room in the US, he expects something more than a history lesson."

"Sam, you're just being overly worried, and I don't understand why. I know you're my greatest well-wisher, but…"

"Dafina, I think you've hurt his feelings."

"Do you really think so?"

"Yes. You let him down."

"C'mon Sam, you're killing me."

"No, I'm not. I just don't want you to get dumped before the relationship even starts."

"Oh Sam, do you really think I've messed up so badly?"

"Yes. That's what I fear."

"You think he's never going to call me again?"

"I certainly don't want to be negative, but I doubt he will."

Dafina frowns and starts crying softly. "To be frank, I got scared. I just got so overwhelmed. All those feelings of guilt and shame and fear that I'm doing something wrong, meeting secretly with a married man and myself being married – it all crashed down on me like an avalanche and broke my back. You both know what my marriage is like: that I don't have a husband but a roommate who's never around, and a business partner who's always abrupt and cranky. Sam, how many times have you heard Hemant lashing out at me? How many times have you told me that nobody else would tolerate something like that? How many times have you told me in front of Kazuo that I'm crazy for being so tolerant and forgiving?"

Dafina tries to imitate Hemant's bossy tone. "'That's not what I'm asking you…You're not answering my question… I don't have time to hear anything! Hurry up, make it quick… You aren't answering your phone…' Telling me that Alec is not going to call me ever again, you made me feel so upset."

"Dafina, that's why I'm saying you shouldn't feel guilty."

"Sam, I couldn't wait to come here and share the good news with you, but you've really spoiled it for me. I thought selfishly that I also deserve some happiness in my life. I fell in love with a gorgeous man, because the one by my side isn't even trying to meet my needs, never ever, and keeps treating me like shit. And you're saying it's already over."

She starts crying even more heavily.

I start laughing.

"You crazy girl, your heart is like that of a small child. Don't you see that I'm just kidding? I'm just playing with you!"

"Sam, it's too late now for those comforting words. Maybe I've really messed up. Maybe Alec will never call back. Maybe our destiny is to be just platonic. And I want to be a source of joy for him, not a burden. I never talk to him about Hemant."

"Sweetie, relax. I was just kidding. I'm sure Alec likes you. You are refreshing for him, you're so different from American women."

"Sam, I'm upset…"

"No need, sweetie, believe me."

"Are you playing with me again?"

"No. I'm serious when I say you shouldn't worry about anything. Everything's good. I'm sure Alec likes you a lot. That he's very happy to be with you."

Dafina lets out a heavy sigh.

"I don't know what to think now. I'm so confused."

"Silly, relax. All is good."

"Whatever, Sam…We'll see in due course of time how things go. I just feel so tired suddenly. Hemant isn't coming home this evening. He'll sleep at his friend's house in Chapel Hill. Can I come here for a sleepover, guys?"

"Of course."

"Thank you. I just don't want to be alone tonight."

"No need to be alone, you're most welcome. No matter what, we're always happy to be by your side," says Kazuo, his first words the whole evening.

Dafina gets up.

"I'll be right back."

After a few minutes, she comes back with her pillow and sleeping bag, her tears almost dry.

"Thank you, guys. I don't know what I would do without you."

LIDIA

Dafina and Hemant are in the courthouse in Raleigh, in the room for child support issues.

After waiting a long time, Hemant's turn arrives.

He's in front of the judge.

He didn't listen to anyone's advice to get a lawyer.

He was counting on the lawyer that he'd get in court, the one who offers free assistance.

He and Dafina try their best to explain the problem to the lawyer, and she seems to understand their situation.

But after a brief conversation with the judge, the judge posts a bail for three thousand dollars, and orders the officers to arrest Hemant.

Two security guards approach him and handcuff his wrists.

Dafina is completely shocked.

She'd never been in a courthouse before meeting Hemant, but because of his ex-wife and her constant accusations every few months, they both became regulars there.

From the lawyer, who obviously didn't help much, Dafina finds out that she must come back with the money to get him out of jail.

She drives like crazy to their friend's house in Cary to borrow some money.

Their friends are also totally appalled. "Why isn't he taking this seriously and cleaning up this mess once and for all? What is he waiting for? Somebody to clean up the shit for him?"

"The tragedy is that he is innocent, but because of his laziness and a few wrong steps along the way, he looks like the most irresponsible father ever. But he has given much more than he was obliged to."

Her friends are kind enough to lend her the money, and Dafina drives like crazy back to Raleigh, so Hemant can be free.

After they let him go, Dafina is very upset, and they go out to dinner at an Indian restaurant.

"I'm a very naïve man," says Hemant.

Dafina thinks, *you think you know everything*, but she keeps it to herself.

"You should sometimes listen to what other people say, because our friends and I definitely wish you well. It's not healthy to be so withdrawn. And, thanks for bringing me to dinner."

DAFINA

I'M NOT WRITING THIS BOOK TO IMPRESS MR. DALTON.

I'm writing it to reveal my soul in front of God, so he can guide me the right way.

I'm writing it to figure out what to do with my life.

I feel like I'm at a crossroads, like a drastic change is coming for me.

I'm excited, scared, but most importantly ready.

Ready to embrace the change.

In due course of time, none of us will be here anymore.

But if God gives me mercy to write an extraordinary book, the book will be here forever.

The book can give solace to the souls who are suffering in a similar way.

It can help them make the right choices.

My plans never work out, but God's plans do.

Let God's desire guide my relationship with Mr. Dalton, which direction it takes, and not my desire or anybody else's.

Writing this book gives me indescribable pleasure, because I often witness the dawn, when night turns to morning, and it's so comforting to be a part of that.

That's my favorite part of the day, because the sky is turquoise-peach, and everybody on earth feels that things are going to be all right.

MR. DALTON

DAFINA IS VACUUMING HER CAR AT THE GAS STATION near to the airport. She is bending, half of her body inside the car.

She is wearing Donna Karan jeans, a Michael Kors shirt and Pedro Miralles shoes.

Her jeans are tight, but because she lost some weight, they come down to the middle of her rear.

She is wearing a Tommy Hilfiger thong, which is half-visible.

Dafina is in a hurry to clean up, because she is supposed to pick up her girlfriend, Brenda, who is flying in from Boston.

She is so focused and doesn't notice that somebody is behind her.

When she turns around, she sees a middle-aged man staring lustily at her.

"You are waiting for the vacuum, sir?"

The man is swallowing her with his eyes.

"Oh, I'm so sorry, sir. I'm almost done."

DAFINA

I'M RUNNING, RUNNING, RUNNING.

I'm speeding, speeding and speeding, to meet my love, Alec Dalton.

To see his beautiful green eyes, to touch his silky ash-brown hair, with some grey on the sides.

To feel him in my mouth.

To give him pleasure like no woman has done before.

He is my inspiration for all good that comes in my life.

He is helping me not only to survive but to blossom and thrive.

I can never pay him back, even in five lifetimes.

Sometimes his face is freshly shaved for our encounters; sometimes he has a beard from a few days.

Either way, he looks stunning.

I make sure to have a fresh bikini wax before we meet, so he can enjoy the smoothness and silkiness of my private parts and thighs.

I love the wrinkles around his eyes and his forehead. It makes him more attractive, sexy and manly to me.

Having Alec in my life means the world to me. I really can't understand how I lived without him.

I thank God every day for sending him my way, every single day.

The first thing we do when we meet in a hotel room is to take off our wedding rings.

We put them aside and cover them with something, so for a few hours we can forget about them.

And before we part, he is putting my ring on my left hand, and I'm putting his ring on his.

Removing the rings is like removing the guilt and forgetting that we are married to other people and not to each other.

Oh, how much I would love to be Mrs. Dafina Dalton, to have a child with him.

Deep down, we are both pious, so it took us a long time to overcome our guilt and get together.

We both believe in karma, and that we were supposed to meet and be with each other.

Somehow, we feel that we are not creating bad karma by getting together but working off bad karma from the past, restoring the balance that was disturbed.

We both believe that God knows about us and will allow us to enter heaven together.

By the way, karma is a tricky thing.

In math, two and two are four. But in the arts and in life, two and two are five.

Not always do goodhearted and beautiful people get good life partners.

Not always do the most educated guys make the most money.

Especially in the US, there are people without a high school diploma who make millions, and guys with PhDs who can hardly make ends meet.

Not always do good and dedicated parents get good children.

Many serial killers had wonderful people as parents.

Hitler's mother was a very goodhearted woman.

My life experience has taught me that the safe players do not always make the best deals.

The people who try to control everything, people who try to predict, they usually get tricked by karma.

I consider myself a safe player, a woman who doesn't like to take risks.

But I've never predicted anything.

When I've tried hard to control something, it usually came out the opposite way.

I never imagined that such a beautiful person as Alec Dalton would live in this deep countryside of North Carolina, in this boring place.

I never thought I would fall for a married guy.

Our encounters mean everything to me.

I never wear lipstick. I never wear perfume before we make love.

I don't want him to go home smelling of Chanel 5, which doesn't go away even after a shower.

Nobody knows about our relationship except God, and of course my best friend Sam and his lover Kazuo.

But they will never rat me out.

Since we got together, I never called Lidia again.

After we make love, I tell him: "You are healing me emotionally. Without you I was lost."

"You're healing me too," he replies with his irresistible half-grin.

I can't help it. I love the guy.

His masculine energy makes me the woman I've always wanted to be.

LIDIA

DAFINA HAS TOLD ME THAT WHEN HER YOUNGER STEP-daughter visits, there is always a lot of tension in the house.

They never know what kind of attitude they'll get from that girl.

The girl still hasn't accepted her. Not yet.

Even after all these years, she still refuses to acknowledge that her dad can be happy with some woman other than her mom.

"I've accepted that I'm still not accepted," Dafina says, "and that's alright with me. You can't force someone to love you."

That's Dafina.

She's very patient and hopes that the girl's heart will one day be transformed, and a beautiful relationship will blossom between the two of them.

Dafina is someone who believes in miracles.

She tries hard to make her stepdaughter's visits memorable.

Besides the other things, she cooks her favorite meals every day, they go to the movies, she does her laundry, she drives her to her friend's houses for sleepovers, and she treats her to frozen yogurt at the girl's favorite shop.

When they sit next to each other, Dafina can feel the uneasiness emanating from the girl.

It's painful. And it's just so painful to pretend that you don't notice.

But Dafina smiles at her, tells her that she's pretty. That she's smart. That she's always nicely dressed, such a wonderful sense of style for a young girl.

She wishes well for the girl.

Then, after a few days, the girl starts speaking about wanting to be back with her mom.

Dafina tells me: "I can understand that. She's at a tender age, and she needs more time to realize that I have nothing to do with her parents being apart. Before I even came into the picture, they'd been divorced for years. Her negativity toward me isn't going to make her parents more compatible."

The elder stepdaughter's visits are different.

The older girl is more tactful, so she doesn't talk about her mother all the time.

She mentions her sometimes, but not in a way to show that she is feeling more comfortable with her than with Dafina.

They always talk about movies.

They're friends.

They love each other.

Dafina tells me she can hardly believe how well they get along.

When the elder stepdaughter saw Dafina the first time at the airport almost seven years ago, she told her: "You're even more beautiful in person. Can I take a picture of you, please?"

Dafina, the hermit, said: "No pictures, please."

They were going to the car, and the girl said: "I want to be tall and beautiful like you. I'd like to have silky hair like you. And I love your accent. You are my newest role model."

Dafina wondered, "Is this for real?"

After few days, the girl says: "I would love you to be my mother."

When Dafina hugs the girl, she feels good.

Dafina loves chocolates and perfumes, books and movies, New York City and her elder stepdaughter's visits.

DAFINA

I'VE TOLD SO MANY STORIES TO MY LOVE ALEC, BUT I'VE never told him about the head priest in our community.

When somebody dedicates his whole life to God, people usually think, "Oh, he didn't have anything smarter to do. He couldn't make it, and so this was his easiest way out."

The life story of Balaram Krishna Goswami couldn't be farther from that.

He comes from an extremely rich family, a Jewish family from Long Island. They own two mansions there, as well as a few luxury condos on Fifth Avenue.

His father used to own private jets and a private island in the Bahamas.

Sometimes in his classes he mentions a funny situation – when he was a child and his mother would scold him about something he wasn't doing right, he would go with their pilot in one of their private jets and take off somewhere, so that his mother would look small from above, powerless to do him any harm, and he would become fearless.

With that example, he teaches us that if we take the shelter of God, we can overcome all our fears and anxieties.

He has an incredible sense of humor.

Everybody loves to be around him, because he makes them so relaxed and comfortable.

As a child, he was always a better student than everyone else.

So, even though his father was a multimillionaire, he earned full scholarships to some of the Ivy League colleges, and ultimately got a bachelor's from Princeton as well as a master's in physics from MIT.

I'm personally always impressed by children in the US who come from mega-rich families but still work hard and earn scholarships fair and square to the most prestigious schools in the country, so that their super-rich parents don't have to pay even a single penny.

Why should you give your daddy a headache by making him pay for your schooling, when there are so many opportunities?

So many immigrants, who don't know the language well, who don't know the school system in the US, who come from the other parts of the world, who are far from their families and friends, they put in their best efforts and they make it here. So why should someone from here, who has all the advantages, not make it?

Even though Balaram Krishna Goswami was surrounded by opulence in every possible way, he became interested in the science of the soul very early in his life.

He felt that soul and matter were two completely different categories. Like so many others in that frame of mind, he started reading tons and tons of books, to figure out the best way to go.

His parents were unhappy with his choice of Hinduism. His mother used to threaten him: "I'm going to get a heart attack because of you. I'm going to die, and it's going to be your fault. You'll be responsible for my early death."

She would tell him that when she was in her early fifties. Now she's in her late eighties and still going strong: swimming, biking, driving and speeding (incidentally, he's mentioned to me that she has the same car as mine), traveling around the globe with her second husband, wearing full makeup and red lipstick, and having lots of fun.

When he visits her on the Upper East Side of Manhattan, she still hopes that he'll give up his preaching and become a doctor.

"I'd like to see you helping people as a doctor, doing something that everybody can appreciate."

She doesn't see the point of his spiritual dedication.

Parents in Macedonia, if they aren't happy with their children's choices in life, say to them: "You are just stirring wind and fog."

His brother has chosen a materialistic way of life, with no interest in spirituality.

When Balaram Krishna Goswami tells him, "You should consider that one day you're going to die, and inquire more about the path of the soul," his brother replies, "Don't spoil it for me."

Balaram Krishna Goswami is a person who loves me unconditionally and is always there for me.

He is my rock in the States.

Sometimes I cry to him impatiently, "When am I going to make it as a writer? When am I going to see my dreams come true?" And he tells me, "God is going to give you incredible material success, if that doesn't disturb your spiritual progress. When you are ready, He will give you what you need… at the right time."

He travels around the globe frequently, but most often to his preaching zones – in the south-eastern US, Sweden, Southern and Eastern Europe, India, Fiji, Australia and New Zealand.

When I e-mail him, he replies within a few hours or, at the latest, the next day.

He knows all my stories. Whenever I feel that I need support or guidance, he comes up with the words that will soothe me the most.

I was an open book to him until I got together with Alec.

I don't have the guts to admit what's going on

with me lately. But I know that he will always be there for me, no matter what. He will never give up on me. He will never reject me or leave me.

Balaram Krishna Goswami is the priest who is giving me instructions in my spiritual path.

About the priest who had given me diksha initiation – which means a spiritual name and formal acceptance into the spiritual order – and who is also very responsible for my spiritual life, I'll tell Alec some other time.

He has an incredible personality, and it's very hard to believe that such people exist on this earth.

SAM

Dafina is supposed to make her signature cake at the temple, because there is some big festival tomorrow, and she's the one who always makes the cakes.

Usually, she makes them with five layers, and they stay in the fridge overnight before being served the next day.

She figured out that they're much tastier that way, than when they're served the same day.

She makes the dough very thin, and the layers very rich and fluffy.

When they mix with each other, the taste is nothing less than heavenly.

She dreams of one day making some of her cakes for the Queen of England for her birthday party.

She's obsessed with kings and queens, and that sort of stuff.

She thinks the world would be a better place if every country were a monarchy, with righteous royals in power.

Dressed in her beautiful magenta sari, she was speeding towards Hillsborough. I'm lying, though. She is not speeding, she is flying. Driving around a hundred miles per hour and overtaking everybody in her way, who slows her down.

When she passed Durham, she heard police sirens behind her and looked in the mirror.

A state trooper. She slowed down and pulled over.

"Oh Lord, help me…"

The state trooper approached her window.

"Young lady, what's going on with you? Do you think you're in an action movie or something?"

Dafina was very embarrassed and kept quiet. She blushed.

"I need your driver's license and insurance, please."

Dafina handed it over obediently. The officer went back to his car.

After some time, Dafina gathered courage and got out of the car.

"Please sir, let me explain…"

The officer shouted, sternly: "Don't get out of your car."

Dafina obediently got back in.

The officer was taking quite a long time, though, so after a while Dafina got out again.

"Sir…"

The officer, this time even more sternly, said,

"You better not get out of your car again."

"Oh, Lord, I'm in trouble," she thought horrified, and got back in.

After filling out some paperwork, the officer approached her window. "So, what was the issue to be in such a hurry?"

"Can I get out of the car now, please?"

After a short consideration, he said, "Sure, if it makes you feel better."

"Thank you, sir," Dafina said and got out of the car, adjusting her sari with her hands. She pulled it down a little, so her feet were completely covered. She was preparing in her mind her performance already. "Sir, I was late for my cooking service in our temple in Hillsborough, and I'm one of the main cooks there not just for Sunday feasts but for the major festivals too and…"

"I apologize, sir. I was so absorbed thinking about the cake I need to make, that I didn't consider how dangerous my driving was. Tomorrow is a very important festival in our temple. I know I did wrong, and I honestly apologize, sir. I feel so embarrassed, but I was totally into the cake, what to put in the dough: dry cherries or dry apricots, which layers I should do first, the buttery or the fruity one, what kind of custard flavor to use: banana or strawberry, and…

I know I made a huge mistake, but my mind was elsewhere, and I know it's dangerous to drive so fast, for me and for everybody else… I truly and sincerely apologize...

I was just afraid that I wouldn't have enough time to do everything I'm supposed to do, and nobody will be there to assist me, I'm supposed to do everything alone, and you know, another cook is coming later to cook for the evening offering, and she's one grumpy lady who doesn't like anybody else in the kitchen, and in our temple we are offering the food to the Deities at the exact time, she cannot be late, and she'll freak out if I'm still there...

"As much as I love to bake, especially to make glamorous cakes, I was so much in anxiety because of the time, and..."

The trooper looked at her with great curiosity. "I think your story is pretty interesting. You say you're a cook, but maybe you should try working as a storyteller. You can really catch your listener's attention."

Dafina blushed.

"Sir, believe me, please. I'm really going to cook. Do you see my outfit? Where else could I go dressed like this?"

The trooper looked her up and down with a half-smile, and for some time didn't say anything.

"I like your outfit, though. It's pretty, and it suits you very nicely."

Dafina blushed even more, but she felt flattered. Too shy though to look at him, she looked down.

Men's lusty glances always made her feel shy.

"This time you're lucky – your story saved you from a ticket. I'll give you only a warning."

"Thank you, sir! Thank you! Thank you."

"And good luck with your cakes. The way you describe them, I wouldn't mind checking it out myself sometime in the future."

"Oh, you are most welcome, sir. Please feel free to come. Every Sunday we have an opulent feast, and delicious meals are served."

He gave her back her driver's license.

"You take care, and don't speed again, okay?"

"Yes, sir. Thank you, sir."

So, that's how my friend charmed the officer.

The only thing that we fight about from time to time is when I scold her for speeding.

"You can't drive like that all the time," I tell her, "It's dangerous."

"You're right, daddy," she mocks me, "but I can't help it."

It's amazing that someone who speeds like that only got one ticket in the last six years. I'd call that a miracle.

There's another story, which is not as flattering as the previous one.

One day Dafina picked up a gentleman from an upper-middle-class neighborhood in Apex, but he was more like a village bumpkin.

When he got into her car, he stank so much of garlic that Dafina was immediately distracted.

She's very sensitive to people's energies and smell.

She was horrified that a professional man in a designer suit and tie, who was supposed to catch a flight in an hour, could allow himself to stink of garlic and not be embarrassed.

Couldn't he have eaten all that garlic two days ago instead?

She's opened her window, but the man insisted that she close them, because he was cold. She thought she'd die from the stench.

Besides, the customer was so harsh and kept harassing her by telling her how to drive, that she shouldn't follow the GPS but go some other way, and that he wouldn't pay her the full fare when he could pay less, because he is no fool and knows a shorter way. He didn't even say 'excuse me' or 'please, ' and Dafina started to hate him on the spot and wanted him to die. She was speeding like crazy just to get rid of him as soon as possible.

On top of it all, he didn't give her a tip.

And on top of that, she got caught speeding to the airport.

But all her seductive charm didn't help her this time, because the police officer was a lady, and that stinky moron was not allowed to get out of the car by the officer throughout their conversation.

Dafina could sense how happy he was that she got into trouble.

She didn't complain about the ticket though and didn't waste any time feeling sorry about herself.

She forgot them both in an instant.

She took it easy and treated herself to a few pieces of beautiful clothing, some perfume, a new Michael Kors genuine leather bag, the third one by that designer in her collection, a manicure and a facial, four books and two CDs from Barnes & Noble, and a nice lunch at her favorite Italian restaurant near our neighborhood.

That day the music there was heavenly, all her favorite songs were playing, and she didn't skip the tiramisu.

LIDIA

Even five months after being released from jail, Hemant still hadn't found time to file a motion at the child support agency that he didn't have his job anymore, as he had been advised to do by everybody: including the judge, the court lawyer, the cashier at the bail office, his close friends and Dafina.

He was busy getting up early in the morning and coming back late at night. His life consisted of driving all day and coming home to eat and sleep.

He behaved like a guest who did not know anything about household matters.

Hemant and Dafina joke all the time that they're great roommates.

"Having an evening at the movies with hubby? Having a picnic with hubby? Having a little relaxed time with hubby with no talk about business?"

Dream on, babe. Dream on.

All of that is science fiction for Dafina.

"If I didn't have my writing, I would certainly go insane. Fortunately, I have my lover, who is always by my side – –and by that I mean my writing," she often thinks.

When Dafina would remind him that time is passing, that he should submit those documents as soon as possible, he'd always say: "Then you drive, and I'll sit at home and take care about filing the motion."

"But Hemant, nobody is reading tarot cards to find out that you lost your job and aren't making the same money as before. It's up to you to inform them. They're not clairvoyants. You must find time. It's urgent. Do you want to go to jail again? It's so hard to understand your leisurely attitude. If I were you, I would have reported it the same day I was laid off, three years ago."

"I don't have time. At least you, if nobody else, can see that I'm never at home."

Dafina was freaking out, but she was helpless. She hates arguments.

"How can he sleep peacefully with all these things unresolved?"

That was the biggest mystery for her.

Soon, a police officer started showing up regularly at Dafina's door, inquiring about Hemant and bringing documents for his arrest. She would try her very best to convince him that they are working on the case, and that very soon all the documents would be submitted.

It looked like the officer believed her. Or maybe he just took pity on her.

MR. DALTON

A LONG TIME AGO, DAFINA MENTIONED TO ME THAT she needs a man's energy, which her husband can't provide. Back then, I didn't understand what she meant.

"Man's energy" in the way of more money? Or better sex?

DAFINA

Dearest Alec, to answer your question: it's neither the first, nor the second one.

When I'm trying everything possible to get pregnant, and all the exams show that I'm completely healthy, and still things don't work out, and then I turn to alternative ways of healing, like herbs and special praying, but my husband still doesn't want to do even a simple sperm test, with the attitude: "They're going to rip me off."

Or he tells me, "If you're not getting a baby, I'm not going to commit suicide. Give me a break."

My mom said the other day: "You're living in one of the world's richest countries. How come you never got medical help in all these years? What are you waiting for? I thought getting a child was your priority. I know that everything is in God's hands, but you should also do something from your side. If you do something, and things still don't work out, at least you'll know that you tried your best. Only in that way you can be at peace. God helps those who help themselves."

A lot of our close friends and family have suggested that we seek medical help, but Hemant always turns a deaf ear.

By the way, I've never wanted to have children just because everybody else has them. It was never a matter of prestige or envy.

Even as a very young girl, I've always had the feeling that raising children is not a game but a huge responsibility, which doesn't always pay back the way you've hoped.

Children are like a lottery; you never know what you're going to get.

Nobody can guarantee that they will bring you good fortune, that they'll become good people, no matter how hard you try.

I never thought that women with children are better than the childless ones. I've met many women with a lot of children who were mean as hell.

Having children makes some women even more envious: "The other children have more of this, more of that… my children don't have…"

But when I got married to the man of my dreams, all my fears disappeared, and I wanted so badly to have a child.

Hemant would often scold me: "You are so obsessed. All your girlfriends notice that too."

I know the main reason for me not getting pregnant again is stress.

We've had stress with his ex and financial matters since day one of my coming to the US.

I've never had the financial security that every woman deep down yearns for.

And still his ex is never happy, even though she got everything.

Never enough given, never enough helped is their attitude.

I definitely need a different man's energy.

When his brother asked him about the miscarriage, why it happened, my husband replied indifferently, "Because of her age," like he was talking about some stranger, not about the person who is supposed to be closest to his heart.

When his ex makes our life hell with all her false accusations about the child support, and tries to make him feel guilty that he remarried, I expect him to fight back, but his attitude is simply, "Well, what can you do?"

And before grabbing my favorite cookbook and giving it to somebody, I expect him to at least ask me, and if I agree, to replace the book for me before he gives it away.

I want a man by my side who will take responsibility to file our federal and state taxes on time. Ours are always filed at the last moment, and never in the proper way.

When I'm down, I would like to hear some words of encouragement, for my husband to hold my hand and tell me: "Don't worry, things are going to be all right."

He usually tells me, "You are mental. Get busy."

How much busier should I get?

All the household chores are on my back.

If one bulb goes out of order, I'm the one to get it and replace it.

I'm helping him the best I can with driving customers.

There were times when I couldn't breathe when I came home, I was so exhausted from work.

I would get up at four thirty in the morning to pick up Mr. Haka, who flies to Zurich, and go out at ten in the evening to the airport to pick up Mr. Ling, who is flying back from Beijing.

I try to maintain some social life, which is necessary for my wellbeing.

To invite friends for dinner as often as I can, no matter that Hemant is never there.

In due course of time, they stop asking where he is. They just ask: "How is he doing?"

"He's always busy. Crazy busy."

I'm doing my spiritual duties. That's my top priority.

I try my best to do my writing, my greatest joy and best way of having an intimate relationship with myself.

When I have a fever, I expect Hemant to bring me a Tylenol, but he usually forgets.

I just feel like he's never there for me, and that my needs, desires and pains don't matter to him.

He's absent physically as well as emotionally. He's an invisible husband, never by my side.

Every single day in the last five years has been

the same. He is out, always on the road.

No weekends, no long weekends, no vacations.

He works almost 24/7, three hundred sixty-five days per year.

I'm tired of going to Christmas and New Year's Eve parties alone. If I don't secure my place somewhere, I'll end up lonely, sitting miserably at home.

I know it's difficult to find somebody who can be entrusted with the phone for more than half a day, who will be a loyal dispatcher.

They all want to be paid good money, and some of his coworkers would be very happy to steal the business in a second.

But who will acknowledge all the sacrifices I've made all these years, before I met Alec?

Who can blame me for falling in love with another man?

The whole humid summer in North Carolina goes by, and we've never made it to the ocean, not even for half a day in the last five years. If nothing else, we could at least enjoy a cup of coffee in some nice café there. In the same way, we've never made it to the mountains in the fall, to admire the changing autumn colors that North Carolina is so famous for.

We don't make it, not because of money but because of time.

No time. Never any time to spend together.

Only work, business, duties.

"That's the nature of the business," he says. "Nobody's there to hold my back. Nobody's there to do the things I'm supposed to do."

I know he's right, but where there's a will, there's a way, as people say.

Even the greatest workaholics in this country find time for their families, for themselves, for fun, for entertainment, for taking it easy.

I wish I were wrong, but this has lasted for too long, more than five years already.

Hemant is not a person you can discuss things with. He shuts you down immediately and withdraws within himself.

And I've learnt a long time ago not to expect more than someone can give.

Therefore, Alec entered my life. He was the consequence, and never the reason. The things didn't start with him, they ended up with him.

I'm still far from being the saint I want to be before I die, but somehow, I don't feel like an adulteress either.

I don't feel that Alec and I are sinners.

He makes me a better person in all aspects of my life, and my heart is full of peace.

I'd rather say that Alec and I are undiscovered saints.

We've found the perfect compatibility between our souls, and there's nothing wrong with that.

We couldn't stop ourselves from connecting.

Sam

I'M GRADUATING WITH HONORS FROM DUKE, AND KAzuo and Dafina are very proud of me.

"This is your second PhD. What's the third one going to be?" Dafina jokes. "I know you aren't going to stop."

She cooks a wonderful dinner for us at her place, and then we catch a Broadway show at the Center for Performing Arts in Raleigh, which Dafina has chosen and Kazuo has paid for.

Later, we relax in a nice bar downtown.

Kazuo and I have scotch on the rocks. Dafina has a Coke.

All evening we laugh and joke, and it's like we've never been in a better mood.

There's a very big change in my life, but I keep it to myself for now. I must do an urban planning project in Morocco for a year, and I'll be leaving in six weeks.

I don't want to spoil it for her.

And I'd like to choose the right words when I tell her, so she can be rest assured that she'll never lose me.

Kazuo is Kazuo, and Dafina is Dafina. They're the two most important people in my life.

I love them to death.

Somehow, I have a feeling that I should tell a few things to Dafina, and that I should tell her tonight.

"Dafina, do you want another Coke?"

"No, I'm fine, thanks."

"Dafina…"

"Yes, dear…"

"You need a man who is very smart, clever, strong, but with a tender side, who knows how to express his emotions, and is supportive in every possible way."

"I think I got that, Sam."

"You definitely don't need some fearful weakling, who will take you for granted, and who will confess to his wife about you after one drink."

"I don't think he would do that. I don't think he wants to lose me. And, by the way, his relationship with his wife is none of my business. If he mentions her, I listen. Other than that, I never ask. I'm not nosy about how he spends his time when he's not with me. I respect his privacy. And I'm very happy when he says something nice about her."

"You need a man who will be careful not to gamble anything that he's already achieved, and who will value you as a precious upgrade in his life, and a man who will not feel scared to see you successful."

"I think Alec is smart, discreet, sensitive, genuinely supportive and… and just the most beautiful person I could hope for."

"You absolutely don't need somebody who will make your life a big mess."

"I don't think I have the luxury to let that happen, Sam. I've suffered enough since I arrived in this country. I don't want to do that anymore. With Alec by my side, I'm learning to love myself again."

LIDIA

Hemant got a customer who is a professional prostitute.

The lady was middle-aged and worn down. Without heavy makeup, she would scare off even the most courageous men.

She catered to elderly men in their sixties and seventies, most of them divorced or widowers. She was drunk most of the time and talked a lot.

Dafina didn't feel comfortable with that, but Hemant didn't care how she felt.

"I'm on the road every day. Times are tough. What do you know about making money? Most of the time you're just reading books."

Dafina is a pathologically private person, but this time she made sure to spread the news to all their friends. Everybody was appalled.

"Isn't he ashamed to be in that kind of company?"

"How can he feel cozy and comfortable with

that kind of person?"

"Are you struggling so much for money that he can't be more selective?"

One day, Dafina invited the head priest home for dinner, so they could discuss the matter with Hemant.

Balaram Krishna Goswami was not at all pleased with the news and said he was very concerned about Hemant.

"Making money from that kind of customer is causing a disturbance in your marriage. And it's not good for your spiritual life, nor for your consciousness. You are obviously not considering how your wife feels about that."

"She is just a customer like everyone else. I bring her from point A to point B. That's a business relationship," Hemant said, trying to present it innocently.

"I don't think she is like everyone else. You know very well what she does for a living, and if she talks about her job, as she does, it's very inauspicious for your consciousness, as well as your marriage."

The head priest instructed Dafina to get some other job urgently, besides driving this lady.

She's tried hard but to no avail, ever since she arrived in this country. But being in the sleepy town of Cary for her field, having no degree or career in the US, no connections, and no powerful friends in high positions, she's never got anything even close to what she had back in Macedonia.

This time she ended up driving the prostitute around most of the time, except at night.

Dafina felt sick to her stomach every time she was supposed to pick this woman up. She was deeply disturbed and felt like vomiting.

"Why are you nagging and complaining? You're getting a good story," Hemant would say coldly.

"Oh, really? Then wait until I get a male prostitute as a customer, who will talk all the time about his job too, so I will have a complete story, with two counterparts. I'd love to see how you feel about that."

It took a whole six months for Hemant to understand that the prostitute was more detrimental than beneficial for their household, financials, and most importantly for their relationship.

He got dozens of speeding tickets and lost his facial glow.

Everybody noticed how drastically he had changed. Not to mention the increasing tension and the uneasiness between them.

In Macedonia there's a saying: "With whom you are, such you are."

He was right about one thing though. Dafina got a good story.

She made sure to always bring her notebook and write down all the phone conversations that the prostitute made with her clients, as well as the talks between them in the car.

Dafina did her best to probe her without seeming too inquisitive or aggressive. She even acted friendly and openhearted to choices that she'd made in life, even supportive at times.

The most intriguing question, which she was dying to get an answer for, was why somebody would start doing that kind of job. What kind of family background, what kind of childhood experiences, traumas or hurts had occurred to send this sad woman so off-track?

She hated the hypocrisy of taking an interest in the prostitute, though, but for the sake of the story she pretended.

"This is going to be a tough story to write, to describe such a miserable life, and still to try to find some meaning in it," thought Dafina. "But when the time comes, I'll try my best, so my readers will not feel as bad as I did listening to her."

DAFINA

Today I got a postcard from Aiko.

She is already in Shanghai, living in a beautiful mansion in an upscale neighborhood, with a lot of Japanese people around.

Her two daughters are with her, and she feels very happy.

I've always admired how she and Kazuo stayed good friends after all the changes in their relationship.

"How are you, Dafina? I already miss you. But it's so beautiful here. I would never move anywhere from here. I finally found my peace. And guess what: I met somebody, but I'll talk to you later about that. Whenever you decide to come to this part of the world, my house and my heart will be open for you."

I'm writing a postcard back to her. "Thank you, Aiko…Your kind words have melted my heart… I'm delighted about the good news…"

And here in Cary, Kazuo is in negotiations to sell the mansion on Giovanni Court.

He's not in a hurry though, because he doesn't want to sell it below market price. So, I visit him often. It's only two minutes by car from my home, and we have drinks and watch TV. Sometimes I cook for him, and we take dinner together. Whenever I visit, we call Sam, and we all talk for a long time. We both miss him dearly, but we are glad that he is working on a project in Casablanca that makes him happy.

I'm very grateful that Kazuo has never showed any impatience about my friendship with Sam, and I never felt that he was jealous.

Just the opposite. On many occasions, he encouraged Sam to be around me, to support me, to go places with me, to offer me his shoulder to cry on.

When he was out of town, he always asked Sam about me, how I'm doing, if I needed something they could help me with.

He is a wonderful gentleman and knows that there is room for both of us in Sam's life, and that our relationships with him are completely different.

I love Kazuo very much too.

I think they are a perfect couple.

After the mansion is sold, Kazuo plans to travel more often to Casablanca, so he can be close to his love.

He is extremely lucky to be so successful and powerful that he can work from any corner of the world with his iPad in front of him.

I miss Sam terribly, I miss our long talks about literature and art, but I know he's happy where he's at, living his dream.

After his assignment ends, Kazuo tells me they plan to move to Manhattan for good.

I'm delighted.

I remember the Macedonian saying, "People who love each other are never separated."

I feel somehow that Sam is always by my side.

That gives me so much strength.

SAM

⟨⟩

JENNY IS AN AFRICAN-AMERICAN WOMAN IN HER LATE fifties who started working for Hemant.

Dafina was visiting her family in Europe when Jenny joined the company.

That was a huge relief for Dafina, because she didn't want to drive so much anymore. She wanted more time for writing.

She is insightful enough to know that if she doesn't push her career forward, nobody will do it for her.

In the last couple of years, though, she got some of the most beautiful and incredible material for unbelievable stories. She is very thankful for the stories and for a long time she has come to believe that driving different people has been the best job that a writer could hope for.

"If I'd worked in some office, I would never get to hear so many interesting confessions. Every day would be more or less the same, which is a disaster for an artist, and for Dafina too."

But, apparently enough driving is enough.

Jenny comes every morning to get the car keys from Dafina and shows up in the afternoon to return them.

So Dafina makes sure to welcome her with fresh coffee, a nice sandwich or juice and candy.

She does everything to make her feel comfortable working for Hemant.

She gives her beautiful gifts: luxurious soaps, lipstick, perfume, fancy notebooks.

Jenny is not very focused and suffers from depression.

Not the best combination for somebody who drives people around, for sure.

And she has some ADHD issues too.

So, she is more off than she is on, which makes the things very difficult for Hemant, and for Dafina too.

Whenever she doesn't show up, Dafina works full-time, like she did before.

After some time, Jenny shared with Dafina that she is a lesbian, and that she loves tall women with long and silky hair.

"Just like you," she said.

Dafina has never had anything against gay people. But these remarks made her feel very uneasy.

Still she managed to say: "Is there somebody for you in your life now?"

"No. I just broke up recently with a woman I've been with for fifteen years."

"I understand. It's not easy, but who knows why things turned that way. Why did you split, if it's not too personal?"

"I'm religious, and she isn't. Because of her, I've neglected going to church all these years. I was so crazy in love with her, and so intimidated that if I did something she didn't approve, she'd leave me. But in the last year I've started going to church regularly again. I've never skipped, not even once, the Sunday morning mass. She couldn't take it, but I didn't want to back off."

Jenny mentioned that she tried to commit suicide twice by swallowing pills but ended up in the hospital with a horrible headache and stomach troubles.

She told Dafina about her childhood, how her father was physically abusive, and how her mother was never there for her.

Dafina listened patiently, day after day.

She didn't mind being her shoulder to cry on.

Many astrologers had told her that she would have made an extraordinary psychiatrist.

Jenny is often complaining about Hemant too, that he's very grouchy, unkind, and lashes out at her.

"He's my worst boss ever."

So many times, she comes in the afternoon looking like a deflated balloon.

"Today, Hemant was picking on me all day long."

Dafina always tries to come up with a nice excuse for him, because she knows that Jenny is not innocent either. So many times, she has messed up trips, and even made some of their regular customers very upset by being late for the pickup.

"C'mon sweetie, don't take it so personally. He's a wonderful man. But he's so overwhelmed. He works day and night. It's not easy to be in his shoes. It's not surprising to be grouchy when you are chronically tired."

One day, Jenny had the audacity to say: "I really don't know how you can live with that man. You're so different."

Dafina felt uncomfortable – it was really none of her business. She felt that Jenny had crossed the line. Still, she was polite and sweet.

"I told you, he has a wonderful heart, and you must understand that he is under a lot of stress. Owning and managing a small business is no picnic – no matter how it might seem from the outside. It's actually very hectic, very demanding. He works very long hours till exhaustion, and at the end of the day, after all the wear and tear that you go through, it's not even for that much money. And remember Jenny, by driving our car, you are always his priority. He gives you the best trips. He cares about you. He wants you to make money. But if you are not in the car, if you don't show up for work, what can he do for you?"

Dafina tries everything to keep her in their company, because if Jenny quits, Dafina will be the one working so hard again.

The next couple of months were like this: Jenny works two days, and the next three days she's off, which means that Dafina must cover the demands of the business.

Jenny always comes up with some excuses – either she is sick, or she must go out of town, she has some emergency with her roommate, she must take care of her grandson, she is supposed to meet a woman who seems to be the real deal this time…

There's a never-ending list of reasons why she is unable to work more regularly.

And she's never worked Saturdays and Sundays, which Dafina understands. In her opinion everyone must find time to unwind. Otherwise, you go nuts sooner or later.

One late evening, Dafina told Hemant: "She's more of a headache than a help. You better let her go."

But Hemant has been patient with her.

When she finally left the company, they weren't surprised. They felt relieved.

It's tough for them, though, because two other full-time employees quit at practically the same time, and only a few of the part-timers are still there.

"To be frank with you, Hemant, I'm really tired of losers working for us. I'm tired of people who can hardly keep their heads above the water. I'm eager to see happy, successful, and joyful faces around me."

DAFINA

After that first encounter with Alec in the hotel, he invited me again.

So, we've chosen another hotel, and met happily there.

The conversation continued as smoothly as if we'd never been apart, not even for a minute.

We talked and laughed and joked…It was magical.

No sex this time, again.

And no sex in the next six encounters either.

In one of those encounters, when I met him in the room, I gave him a hug and kiss and then fell asleep. I felt so tired because I had slept only two hours the previous night.

When I woke up, he was lying next to me, gently fondling me.

He looked so cute at that moment.

Alec is obviously a very patient boyfriend. He felt that I was still not ready.

He was happy to just listen to me talk.

He felt relaxed and somehow grateful that we could just spend time together, without being interrupted by anybody.

That's what our meetings in the hotel rooms are: we create our own world, our own secret paradise, which gives us strength to endure the problems of our everyday life.

I never got the impression that he gets irritated that he has paid for the room and nothing physical happens.

He never gets an attitude or loses his temper.

He's proven to be a gentleman par excellence.

On our eighth encounter besides the talking, I gave him a foot massage.

On our ninth encounter, I gave him a blowjob and pleased him extraordinarily. He told me that I was the best.

On our tenth encounter, I opened my legs to him and he'd made love with me like there was no tomorrow.

From that moment on, our sex was madness, out of this world.

LIDIA

Sam is still in Morocco, working diligently on his urban planning project.

Kazuo is in Hong Kong, having meetings with his executives from Japan and China.

Alec is in London with his family, visiting his parents.

Hemant is on the road all the time as usual, but one night he makes a big exception.

He accompanies Dafina to her graduation from Barbizon Fabulous, a reputable school that she's attended for the last seven months.

The event is held at the Center of Performing Arts in Raleigh in the evening, but all the students are obliged to come in the morning, so they can practice their choreography and stage setting.

Dafina is going to get her certificate for Modeling and Acting.

Her group's turn to perform comes at the end of the event.

She is wearing beautiful black boots with high heels that come above her knees, a black lace dress by Calvin Klein and an ivory pea coat by Michael Kors.

Her make-up and hair are impeccable. She looks like a model from a magazine.

After all the performances are done, the winners are announced.

The main awards are going to be the first, second, and third place for the book called "Model Magic Magazine", a project that all the students were obliged to prepare, and without which nobody can graduate.

It contains a lot of mandatory articles and covers all the topics that were presented from the beginning of the courses till the very end.

After announcing the minor awards, it came time to present the winners for the "Model Magic Magazine".

Dafina was disappointed to get second place but hid it perfectly behind her beautiful smile.

She had hoped her book would be recognized as the best.

First place went to a girl whose father was a millionaire, and whose book was not even close to being as good as Dafina's.

Dafina was the only foreigner in the school; all the other sixty students were Americans.

Apparently, the owners of Barbizon Fabulous thought that if they gave the first award to the daughter of a wealthy man, he might sponsor the school.

Boy, did they get that wrong.

Not only didn't he show any interest in helping the school, but his daughter unfriended both owners from her Facebook account.

They never crossed paths again.

DAFINA

Where are you flying, sir?

Madrid.

Where are you flying, sir?

Paris.

Where are you flying, sir?

Buenos Aires.

Where are you flying, sir?

Rome.

Where are you flying, sir?

Rio de Janeiro.

The other day I met a gentleman from Moscow. He was in a hurry for his meeting, so he asked me to speed from the airport to his company, which I gladly did.

I told him I've been to Moscow a few times, a long time ago.

"There must be a very different atmosphere nowadays, sir."

"That's true. Life is much better than before."

He looked quite content.

We talked about many famous Russians who made it very big.

Every day I have so many encounters with different men. To be frank, I'm getting tired of it.

Yesterday I brought a gentleman who was from Ohio to the airport, and he told me that he's on the road forty weeks of the year.

"This routine has lasted for two decades already."

"Aren't you exhausted from so much traveling, sir?"

"No, I enjoy it."

He tells me that his wife passed away long time ago, and his children are grown up, so he has found peace of mind in his work.

Five times per year he flies to Europe.

He's amazed by the European culture and lifestyle, and tells me that if he could afford it, he would like to move there for good.

"It's beautiful there," I say. "The only disadvantage is that Europe is very costly. You must have a lot of cash to live a decent life."

"Yes, that's how things are there," he says.

Today I had to bid farewell to a German gentleman. I used to take care of him for the whole month. In the morning I'd bring him from his hotel to the company, and in the afternoon again back to the hotel.

He was from Hamburg, a mechatronics expert,

but he knew a lot about the arts.

We talked about literature, theatre, classical music, and opera.

It somehow happened that we love the same German writers, as Thomas Mann, one of my three favorites of all time. He was a Lutheran Christian.

Also, we admire the same book, Thomas Mann's Buddenbrooks.

Long time ago in India, during my first visit there, an astrologer told me that I'd been a German in a previous lifetime, as was my whole Macedonian family.

No wonder.

I've learned German from the first grade in the elementary school.

Everybody in my family speaks it, and my mom used to teach high school German at the beginning of her career.

The money for building the school that I attended - which was the most beautiful, by the way - was donated by the Swiss government, as a gift to the City of Skopje after the disastrous earthquake of 1963.

Many of my teachers were German too. I used to speak the language much better than I speak English now, and without an accent.

Since then I have always felt a very deep connection to the German culture.

As a very young girl I started to admire the mentality of the progressive people who had the guts to turn against Hitler, and who felt embarrassed that he brought such a shame to their country.

I loved their writers, their composers, and their theatrical achievements, and felt ashamed about the Nazis.

During my few business visits to Berlin, I felt like I had finally found my home.

A few days before he was supposed to fly back, the gentleman from Hamburg told me that he missed his dog more than he missed his wife.

"Still, I made sure to buy a lot of gifts for my wife."

"That's so wonderful, sir. I'm sure she will be very happy."

He thanked me very politely for taking such good care of him and said that he was very happy with me.

"Thank you, sir."

"Maybe I'll see you again. I'm coming at the end of the fall."

If he comes, I secretly hope that some miracle will happen in my life by then, and that I'm not going to be in this business anymore.

SAM

———————⟨∞⟩———————

Owning a small transportation business like Hemant's and Dafina's means that you never have your own peace. The business is open 24/7, which means that anybody can call anytime, day or night.

Hemant can never take his mind off work. Neither can Dafina.

In the last couple of years, she hardly took her lunch or dinner without being interrupted by a phone call from Hemant, asking her to go on some trip.

She's never read a book or watched a show without being interrupted.

When she sits in front of her laptop, either writing or just browsing, again there are interrupting calls all the time.

When she talks to her friends on the phone, Hemant calls on the other line.

Even when she goes to take shower, she takes

her phone into the bathroom.

"I can't go to the restroom peacefully anymore because of you," she jokes with him.

Time for a vacation, babe?

You better forget it.

Fortunately, she reads books all the time, so she travels vicariously around the world from the comfort of her sofa.

If you ask her to describe a piece of paradise, she'll say: "Reading a great book on the daily light, sitting comfortably next to the window."

Recently she was in Chile, later in Honolulu, after that in Paris, and then Egypt.

The last book she read brought her all around Canada.

Their schedule is not only hectic, it's crazy.

"It's good to learn new things," Dafina says often. "My time flies. I never feel bored, and that's my good fortune."

She has something adventurous in her, but still dreams about a time when they will be able to wrap up their business and live off of her writing.

"I've got enough stories for now, I think."

Hemant is very professional, always on time, very polite, and a good provider.

He has a great sense of humor, and everybody thinks he's the sweetest guy in the world, especially from the messages he leaves:

Dear Mr. Robbins,

Thank you very much for your message,

We've made all the changes to your itinerary. We'll be there for you.

Thank you for your business.

With kind regards,

Hemant Kumar

LIDIA

DAFINA HAS A CUSTOMER NAMED DOTTY, A RICH EL-
derly lady originally from New York City, and a widow
without children.

Her nephew takes care of her financials and
arranges everything for her.

Being a communicative person, Dafina tried to
start a conversation when they first met, but to no
avail.

Whatever Dafina asked, Dotty didn't know or
couldn't remember.

Every day except Sunday, Dafina brings her
from her home to the same restaurant so she can
take her lunch there.

In the meantime, she goes to Barnes & Noble,
sips her drink peacefully and reads some book or
magazine.

It's a very relaxed time of the day for her.

In that bookstore, she feels like a fish in the
water.

Then when Dotty is ready, she brings her back home.

Every day the elderly lady has the same lunch: fried chicken with okra, salad, iced tea and apple cobbler.

On the second day, Dafina tried talking to Dotty again, but the old woman simply didn't respond.

"Is she very reserved or just stupid?" Dafina wondered.

The ride takes about six to seven minutes.

In that period, Dotty would ask her at least five times what day of the week it was.

Dafina would reply, and then one minute later Dotty would ask the same question.

Dafina would reply again, very patiently. And this happened on every trip.

Or she'd ask: "Did you talk to my nephew?"

"No, I didn't."

After a minute: "Did you talk to my nephew today?"

"No dear, I didn't."

It wasn't hard for Dafina to figure out that Dotty suffered from dementia.

So, Dafina started being playful with her instead, and it looks like it's working out better.

They laugh and have a good time in the car.

No matter how crazy she is, Dotty never misses a chance to tell Dafina that she looks beautiful and that she is nicely dressed.

After a couple of years, the elderly lady showed

up in the driveway using a walker. She could walk perfectly though.

"Why do you need a walker, Dotty?" Dafina asked.

"Where have you been? I've used my walker every day since the morning you'd first picked me up."

"Oh, okay. Sure."

So, from that day on, even if she doesn't take the walker from her home, she demands that it be given back to her.

"But you never took it with you, my dear. How can I give it to you?"

"You're hiding it in the trunk, I'm sure about that, and I'm ashamed of you. And I don't like to be ashamed of people."

Dafina doesn't get angry. She feels very sorry for her, though, because her condition worsens every day.

She can see craziness in Dotty's eyes, and it breaks her heart, because Dotty is a goodhearted lady.

Very often Dotty tells her on the way back: "A man brought me this morning, and he was very nice."

It was Dafina who brought her to the restaurant, but she defers to Dotty on this.

"Oh yes, I know him. You're right, he is very nice."

Among Dafina's regular customers, only

Yvonne, Kimberly and Mr. Dalton know that she's a writer.

All of them are very supportive and wish her luck.

Only with them she can talk about what she is currently reading, and what she is writing.

Dafina rarely tells anyone about her life and her most precious dreams.

MR. DALTON

DAFINA USED TO LIVE IN THE DOWNTOWN OF SKOPJE, only a half minutes' walk from the main square, which is named after Alexander the Great.

Just next to her residential building was the high school from which she and her sister both graduated. It was the most prestigious school at that time.

Between the building and the high school is a lawn with a small fence.

From their sixth-floor apartment they could easily see all the classrooms, which have huge windows. If you were to toss something from their living room in the direction of the school, it could easily land on one of the balconies outside each classroom.

When they were absent from school, they could see their classmates sitting or standing up to reply to the teachers.

The other day, Dafina told me that in all four

years of her schooling, her dad never went to inquire about how she was doing, not even once.

In fact, he wasn't even sure which grade she was in. She'd have to remind him from time to time.

Recently, when she talked to her sister, who is older than her, she asked: "Do you remember if dad ever went to inquire about us, ever?"

"No, he never did."

"Are you sure?"

"Positive."

He was a very busy guy, but she and her sister love him to death.

DAFINA

A FEW GOLDEN RULES FROM MY MOM: NEVER LEAVE THE house without wearing eyeliner, lipstick and perfume.

Always dress nicely.

And polish your shoes at least twice a day, so there is never even a little dust on them.

You can estimate a person's culture according to the cleanliness of their shoes.

Therefore, I ended up polishing my shoes diligently all my life.

"Remember Dafina, even if nobody's there on the streets, the sky is always looking at you."

"All right, mom. I'll remember."

I apply these rules religiously, no matter where my life has brought me.

Now when I'm driving people, I refresh my make-up at least five or six times a day.

People appreciate my appearance. The way I look when I take care of them, they feel respected, that they're important to me.

Many gentlemen have told me that I don't look like a limo driver at all.

They were shocked when I went to pick them up the first time.

I ask them: "How do limo drivers look?"

One gentleman from Portugal was so perplexed when he saw me, that he hesitated to get into my car for quite a while.

I turned my head left and right and asked him:

"Do you see somebody else here for you, sir? Do you want to miss your flight, or will you take a chance and ride with me after all?"

Many times, it has happened to me that a gentleman is waiting in front of a company and they don't figure out that I'm their ride.

I rarely talk about my real profession, so for most of my customers I'm an enigma. It's quite difficult for them to reconcile my energy with my role as their driver.

For a struggling writer, I'm doing quite well though.

I never have less than forty designer perfumes. When I become bored and realize that I will not be able to use them in the next five years, I bring half of my perfumes to my mom when I go back to Europe.

A long time ago I told Hemant not to buy me any more perfumes, but he always does. So, I guess my destiny is to have plenty of them.

Looks like there's no redemption for me in that

regard.

I scold him for buying me perfumes, but I buy them for him all the time too. So, he has many bottles also.

SAM

I'VE BEEN IN MOROCCO FOR ALMOST A YEAR. CASABLAN-
ca is great, and I've met terrific people here. I've worked
very hard, though, and can't wait for a break.

Kazuo has been visiting me twice a month. We
had great time traveling through the northern part
of Africa, but I wish Dafina were here with us too.

Still I'm not sure if I'd want to return to this
part of the world in the future. But you never
know. I never dreamed that I'd end up here.

There have been some big changes in our lives.

Kazuo finally sold his mansion on Giovanni
Court for a very good price.

A couple from Norway bought it.

Both sides were very happy with all the ar-
rangements.

When the transaction was done, he got an
apartment on Fifth Avenue, in the building where
Jacqueline Kennedy used to live.

After my assignment is over, we're moving to

Manhattan. No more North Carolina for us.

Kazuo moved the business from Raleigh to Manhattan. So, nothing's keeping him back.

When I tell Dafina, I'm sure she'll be thrilled for us.

I hope she's keeping her head above the water.

She's proved to be resilient so far, and last time we talked on the phone, she told me that Alec was being very good to her.

"He is my sunshine," she said. "I'm very blessed."

LIDIA

More than four years ago, Hemant lent around five hundred dollars to a coworker who was originally from Gambia. The man pretended to be very sweet and acted like his best friend.

He never returned the money though.

A year and a half ago, Hemant entrusted the same man with two thousand dollars more.

Again, he got burned. He never saw that money again, and the Gambian man vanished for good.

MR. DALTON

DAFINA HAS INSTRUCTED ME IN A VERY POLITE WAY that I should dress casually for our encounters in the hotels.

"Please, no luxurious designer suits, shirts, ties, and shoes. You are too conspicuous that way. Everyone turns to look at you."

I think she is right, no need for extra attention.

So, I dress in jeans, casual shirts and sneakers.

She does the same, but when we get in the room, she changes into some gorgeous dress that she brought in her bag.

Even after being together for so long, I still can't convince her that we should meet more often.

She tells me: "The chemistry between us is great, the sex is the best I've ever had, but your beautiful soul is what I'm most in love with."

My girlfriend is stubborn but irresistible.

Since we never go anywhere, and I don't spend

anything on her, from the beginning of our encounters I've started to give her money. Nothing much, just a couple of hundred dollars.

She's never asked me for that, and at first, she felt slightly uncomfortable.

"I never bring you anywhere, because you never allow me to. So, you can just buy something for yourself. I want you to have some nice memories, some nice gifts from me."

But she doesn't listen and doesn't spend even a penny on herself.

Instead, she gives all the money to the temple in Hillsborough, but always secretly. When nobody is there in the temple room, she puts it quietly in the donation box.

A very small amount she donates to the Catholic Church in Apex, where she attends the Saturday evening mass with Ms. Yvonne, when she's not at the movies.

Dafina's paternal grandparents were Orthodox Christians, and her maternal grandparents were Catholic. So, she is familiar with both sides, because as a young girl she attended both churches in her hometown.

She tells me: "Fifty percent is atonement money, so if there is something we should be forgiven for, we'll be forgiven for sure. The other half is for our spiritual advancement."

On many occasions when my family has been out of town, I've invited her to my house.

She's never accepted the invitation though.

"Let it be how we are, my dearest," she tells me and kisses me gently.

But she cooks for me from time to time and brings dishes to the hotels when we meet. I do really enjoy her cooking.

DAFINA

From the fall of 2007 until the end of the next year, I've been working on my third novel, usually from ten at night until five in the morning.

It is a very quiet time for writing, when everyone in North Carolina is pretty much asleep.

Until Hemant started with his transportation business at the end of February 2008, he used to help me with the cooking, and I was grateful for that.

He is a wonderful cook, and very talented, and besides delicious Bengali cooking, he can prepare Italian, Chinese, Swiss and Mediterranean meals perfectly.

He makes the best pizza in the world.

LIDIA

Hᴇᴍᴀɴᴛ ᴄᴀʟʟᴇᴅ Dᴀғɪɴᴀ ᴀɴᴅ ɪɴᴠɪᴛᴇᴅ ʜᴇʀ ᴛᴏ ᴛʜᴇ Hilton Garden Inn near the airport, so he could see her beautiful face.

Dafina was excited.

Maybe he had a nice surprise for her, she thought.

Their seventh anniversary was approaching.

Some romantic trip out of town (it's been forever since they've traveled together somewhere), or maybe a box with glamorous jewelry is awaiting her.

"Who knows. Looks like Hemant has finally realized how much he has neglected me all these years. Maybe, it's dawned on him that he hasn't been treating me well at all.

Maybe he feels that somebody else is in my life, and if he doesn't change his attitude soon, he'll lose me for good," she wondered.

She came to the Hilton, and the first thing

Hemant told her is that there was no money left in their checking account.

"How come? What happened?"

"I've wanted to pay my dinner and the card didn't go through."

That was the evening before Thanksgiving.

The morning after, he told her that the IRS hadn't accepted his Offering of Compromise and that they were in debt around one hundred and twelve thousand dollars.

Dafina was dumbstruck.

"How come so much? The way you presented the situation I thought it would be just a couple of thousand?"

Hemant: "Interest, penalty."

Dafina: "What?"

Hemant: "It's karma."

Dafina: "Karma?"

Dafina completely freaked out.

"Karma?! I don't think so. That's negligence. It's ignorance. It's conceit to think that you know everything the best. I'm the witness to how you've ignored the whole thing all these years, how you refused to take proper care... Whenever some letter comes from them, I've never seen you, not even once, take it seriously. And all this shit is from long before I even met you. Why should I suffer from your wrongdoings? How many times have we fought about this, because I felt something was wrong, but coming from another country, I've been ignorant myself too! How many times I've begged you to start fixing this mess, and told you I don't feel comfortable reminding you again and again… I believed you that you could fix it. But you always procrastinated, saying you were too busy running a business and had no time to bother with them. What did you think, you could outsmart the government? That they would forget about your debt and just forgive you? They'll kill you with the penalties! It's like injecting cancer into your body voluntarily, so in due of course it can destroy you for sure. It's like throwing away thousands of dollars just for fun, because you don't have anything smarter to do. It's like a rabbit covering his eyes with his ears and refusing to acknowledge the wolf right there in front of him, ready to swallow him up. You gave me so much pain and suffering with your disastrous dealings with the financials, I really don't know how much more I can take. You act like you came to this country yesterday, like you don't know how things work. After living here for almost thirty years, you should know better… Why have you always had so many problems with financial matters? You work hard, you're educated… If you're so busy or don't feel comfortable dealing with it, then hire a professional to help you… There are tax offices on every corner. Again, by trying to save a couple of hundred dollars, you're losing thousands… I understand that we make mistakes… nobody's perfect… But to repeat the same mistakes again and again, that I can't understand… Maybe I'm a bad person for you, maybe I'm a bad influence…"

Hemant: "Don't take it personally."

Dafina; "Oh Lord, please help me cope with this man…"

Hemant: "What's wrong with a man who works day in and day out to support your household?"

Dafina: "To support my household?" she laughed bitterly. "You make me laugh after all. We're taking one step forward and two hundred steps back. Making a little money with a lot of hard work, with a lot of blood and sweat, and throwing away so much more…Since I came to this country, I've faced only stresses and shocks. It's a miracle that I give the impression to everybody who comes my way that I'm the most joyful woman in the world with not a care in my life. I've never considered myself a good actress."

After a few days, Hemant told Dafina that they also owe around twenty-five thousand in state taxes.

She thought: "Where is Alec now to hold me, to kiss me, to make love to me, to tell me to stay positive? I just need to see his beautiful eyes, and to hear from him that he's hundred percent sure that I'm going to make it."

Dafina would never say any of this to her love. She doesn't like anybody feeling sorry for her, least of all her beloved………

So how does she find solace? By remembering her dad's saying: "There is always a solution for everything."

She is already thinking of writing an Oscar-winning comedy about a guy who is nice but is completely lost in the universe. She starts laughing, imagining funny situations on the big screen…

SAM

WHENEVER DAFINA'S FAMILY AND FRIENDS HEAR ABOUT the latest financial disaster, their reaction is pretty much the same.

They're shocked, horrified and speechless.

Then everybody asks the same questions: How could he let this happen?

What was he thinking?

When the warning letters arrived all these years, what did he do?"

Dafina: "Nothing. He would say, 'I'll talk to them… I'll negotiate with them…' And then he'd forget about the whole thing five minutes later. He'd say, 'I'm too tired. I can't do this.'"

Some of her friends with sharper tongues would ask:

"Is he autistic?

Does he have some mental illness that prevents him from thinking rationally about what he's supposed to do to function in society?

Is his business just an excuse for him to avoid household duties? To be aloof and distant and indifferent because it suits him better?"

One of Dafina's friends told her: "He looks like a guy who is capable of making the world wonderful for everyone around him."

Dafina: "I know. Everyone tells me: 'Your husband is so sweet, so nice. You are such a lucky woman. ' I tell them. 'He is wonderful…' So many people think that he's the good guy, and I'm the restless one. That I'm the one who's wild at heart."

In the next couple of months, Dafina ran in every direction trying to fix the blunder.

She met regularly with her girlfriend, who is a lawyer, and followed her instructions religiously.

Her friend was a German lady, born and raised in Munich, named Sabine.

Sabine was actually one of Dafina's best girlfriends.

After Sabine's mother remarried, they moved with her stepfather to the States because of his job.

She was only fifteen at the time.

When they meet, they always talk about Europe: how much they miss it, how Europe is a lot of fun, and how they'd like to visit more often.

Sabine is a real stunner: tall, beautiful and extremely smart.

Dafina was so proud when she found out that they shared the same horoscope sign.

Sabine is one year and four days older than Dafina.

Fortunately, she is always there for her, always.

Even if Dafina calls her in the middle of the night, Sabine, who lives in Apex, gets in her car and comes over to help.

So many times, Sabine has left her husband and her two-year-old son at home and stayed for a sleepover at Dafina's.

In the meantime, Alec began to feel anxious, because whenever he called her, Dafina didn't seem to have time for him anymore.

MR. DALTON

I'M AFRAID THAT MY SWEETHEART HAS MET SOMEBODY else.

I bet some guy who is richer than me, with more connections, more capable of giving her a hand.

Some single guy, how they say in Macedonia: "A man without luggage…"

We haven't seen each other for almost three months.

Whenever I call, she's in the middle of something. She sounds nervous and anxious, and doesn't seem happy to hear from me. She's always in a hurry.

She tells me: "I'm going through a pretty rough time, my dearest. I'll talk to you later. I'll call you back, I promise. I miss you so much. I love you. You are the man of my life."

And then she never calls me.

I think she's fooling me.

Lately, she has been very neglectful and even insolent towards me.

DAFINA

I HAVE TWO FAVORITE MAGAZINES IN THE US: *The New Yorker* and *Vogue*.

It finally dawned on me what Hemant suffers from.

Recently in *The New Yorker*, I came across an article about post-traumatic stress disorder.

All the cases helped me to understand this condition that I recognize now in him.

Hemant told me that long before his formal separation from his ex-wife, he realized that he didn't love her anymore.

He prayed to God to help him out of that marriage. But his attachment to his children kept him from leaving.

When he moved to North Carolina, everything was new for him.

And his ex did everything she could to make his relationship with the kids as difficult as possible.

He's endured a lot of financial harassment, emotional and verbal abuse, and all sorts of torture.

He's faced a lot of negativity from her, and struggled enormously.

That was the year when he started messing up with the taxes.

When we met five years after that, he looked like somebody who had gotten himself pretty much together.

He was joyful, full of life, dynamic and creative.

Everything looked wonderful for us.

But just a few months after we got married, he lost his job.

That hit him very hard.

He was no longer capable of offering me the life he wanted for me, and he became very withdrawn.

He started to lie, to pretend, to hide his real situation from everybody, and more importantly from me. He became passive and lethargic.

Seeing him all these years so different from the man I'd fallen in love with, I couldn't understand how I misjudged his character so drastically.

I'm aware that every person has more or less a double nature, that we all have our good side and our dark side.

But he just acted so incredibly different back then.

Everything happens for a reason, though, as

they say in this country.

I don't have any regrets.

If I didn't suffer so much, God would never have sent Alec my way.

For more than three months, I felt unprepared to meet with my love.

I didn't want him to see me in such a bad condition.

I didn't want to tell him what I was going through.

With him, I wanted to be 'Dafina the Mover,' 'Dafina the Shaker,' 'Fantastic Dafina,' 'Terrific Dafina'…

Always and forever.

He had enough on his plate, and I was very grateful for what he has always offered me ever since the first time we got together.

SAM

Dafina has moved earth and sky to help Hemant again.

She worked tirelessly with Sabine to settle his state and federal taxes.

Now Hemant is supposed to pay a certain amount every month, so there's no danger that they'll put him in jail.

She's realized, though, that it's finally time to start thinking about her own needs.

So, she packed her favorite books, clothes, perfumes and jewelry, and she is about to move in with us.

Kazuo and I miss her cooking.

And there's enough room for her here.

We love her dearly.

We'll have a great time together.

She explained to Hemant that she needs some time for herself, to think about what she wants to do with her life.

They are separating like friends. No bad blood. No hard feelings.

Even Hemant has told her, hundreds of times, that nobody will come knocking on their door and asking to publish her books. So many times, he has told her to be brave and just get out there.

I'm sure Alec will give his blessings and good wishes about her move too.

She is meeting him this evening after more than three months. I'm sure she's more than a little excited.

DAFINA

Aｆｔｅｒ ｃｏｕｐｌｅ ｏｆ ｍｏｎｔｈｓ ｏｆ ｈｅｌｌ, I ｔｈｉｎｋ I ｄｅｓｅｒｖｅ a piece of paradise.

So tonight, I'm meeting with the love of my life.

In the last couple of years, more than twelve hundred men have been in my car.

The last customer was a lady.

I'm waiting at the gas station near the airport so when Hemant calls me, I can go and pick her up.

This is the last time I'm helping with the driving.

Tomorrow morning, I'll be gone.

I'm walking around my car and doing some extra prayers on my prayer beads.

One stunningly good-looking man, strawberry blond with green eyes stops by my side and asks if I need help with anything.

I say I don't and thank him and continue my

praying.

It's kind of weird that he approached me.

I didn't think about men. I didn't think about sex.

I had a completely different vibe.

Doing my praying, I've thought about God and the spiritual world that is above heaven.

The lady I'm picking up is from Johannesburg, South Africa.

She is very sweet and well-spoken, so we talk all the way to her hotel.

I ask her name.

She tells me 'Karabo Tshepo,' and explains what that means in Tswana.

'Karabo' means 'answer,' and 'Tshepo' means 'hope.'

She is really good news, and I enjoy having her company.

Hemant and I have already said our goodbyes.

He will spend the night at his friend's house in Chapel Hill.

It's too painful for him to see me leave.

After all, we've had some beautiful moments together too.

On this night, Alec and I are breaking the rule that's been in place since we started our encounters.

We are dressing up the best we can. No need to hide anymore.

No more encounters in North Carolina.

I can't wait to feel him inside me again.

It's been so long, and I'm so sorry I caused him so much suffering by not explaining what was going on in my life.

He has a nice surprise for me too.

When we meet, he tells me that he has sent his family out of town on vacation, so he can stay the whole night with me. Then in the morning, he'll give me a ride to the airport.

I'm delighted. It's such a relief not to be in a hurry.

My love is standing in front of me and I'm on my knees.

I'm giving him a blowjob like there's no tomorrow.

He is stroking my silky hair with his hands, enjoying it tremendously.

That's what makes me the happiest.

He tells me that he loves me to death.

Oh, how much I love his smell and his flavor.

There is something very sexy about being submissive to the man of your life.

Alec has always been in charge, and I've loved that feeling.

We make love the whole night, and it's madness.

We both know this is our last encounter in North Carolina.

Alec is giving me a ride to the airport.

I'm sitting next to him.

He's speeding.

I'm pinching his arm gently. "I don't want to die."

He's enough of a gentleman not to say: "See how it looks."

When we separate, I start to cry.

I'm looking at the clouds and the sun. It's a gorgeous view.

The lady next to me is sleeping peacefully.

So many stories I've never told my love.

The story about the thief and the brahmana, the one about the ballerina from the Greenwich Village who had a multi-millionaire painter for a husband, the story about how I have around forty children, smaller and bigger (my scripts), stories about my hypnotherapy regressions…

The story about how I feel like my soul and my body are like a beach, and his soul and his body are like an ocean, and that we can never be separated.

Then I think back to when I picked him up for the second time.

I'm not nervous, because I know who he is, and I've learned the directions, so I'm not going to need help from my GPS.

Hemant has always instructed me to be early, adding: "Customers appreciate that."

I don't know how much longer I'm supposed to wait, so I sit in the back, because there's more space for my long legs, and I start reading a book. I always have a book in my car.

He comes out of his house and greets me cheerfully:

"Good Morning, Dafina."

I'm delighted that he remembers my name.

"Good morning, Mr. Dalton."

He asks me why I'm sitting in the back.

I don't remember exactly what I'd replied to him.

He asks: "How are you?"

I smile politely at him. "I'm good, thank you." That's not exactly true, though, because I had just gotten my period and feel very weak and groggy. but of course, I can't tell that to a man I hardly know. You don't tell something so personal to a stranger.

The ride to the airport is very pleasant. We talk about many different things, and the conversation is very easygoing.

It's obvious that we like each other's energy.

When we reach the terminal, he tells me he'll be back on Thursday at noon.

I look at his handsome face.

"I will be here," I say. "I'll be here for you."

THE END

Cary, North Carolina

Join my Mailing List to get a FREE short story!

www.AnaShapkaliska.com

You'll also get monthly updates on the next book in this series, and other stand-alone novels.

Read on for an excerpt from my next novel:

East Boston Blues

EAST BOSTON BLUES

A Novel by Ana Shapkaliska

Part One

There were three things about Manuel that made Hariklia fall madly in love with him. They first met through the Internet in March 2004.

She lived on the prestigious Macedonia Street in downtown Skopje, and he lived in Boston. Her apartment was above the Baldinini – a store that sold Italian shoes. Despite the building being old and the apartment being small and squalid, Hariklia proudly considered herself a city girl. She'd often go to the Barcelona café across the street for a cappuccino. She particularly liked to sit facing the City Museum of Skopje from where she could enjoy the view of the setting sun over the hills of Vodno. On TV, she liked watching the sun set magically on exotic islands around the world. She'd never been

to those places, but she found the sunsets in Skopje romantic enough for her.

Occasionally, she'd stop by for lunch nearby
at Pelister, a restaurant on the main square. She
especially liked their pizza with mozzarella and ol-
ives, their pinjur (spread made from peeled roasted peppers, tomatoes and eggplant spiced with
ground garlic, parsley and steaming hot sunflower
oil), chocolate cake and banana frappé.

Ever since she was a little girl, her mother had
called her 'Hari'. And since then, she was known by
that name to all her relatives and friends, well-wish-
ers, neighbors and colleagues. Anyone who knew
her, called her 'Hari'.

As one of the most gifted and talented students in her class, Hari graduated from the Cyril
and Methodius University in Skopje with honors in
literature. She often wrote fiction, which she kept
in a small leather-bound book, and she dreamt of
becoming a world-renowned author one day. Some
Macedonian writers were considered national trea-
sures, but rarely did their fame ever reach beyond
the national borders. Hari wouldn't want that destiny for herself. She didn't desire the writing career
of a local hero. She longed for the time when her
translated books would flood the entire world and
people far and wide would enjoy the creations of
her mind.

She did not belong to any political party although, in Macedonia, people with a political en-

gagement enjoyed more successful careers than those who were politically inactive. She got several offers to join the various parties, but she turned them all down. Many people thought that, with this kind of attitude, she was signing on to be a loser.

When she graduated, there were no teaching positions open at the university, and she felt that it wasn't her calling to be teaching middle and high school students, so she avoided applying for administrative jobs, knowing well that it would suffocate her creative soul. So, rather than sitting at home without a job and being dependent on her retired mother, for thirteen years, she worked downtown at Adam's movie rental store. The store's owner, Riste, was her high school buddy. Her salary was quite respectable according to Macedonian standards – about twice the national average.

Adam's had all the latest American and European movies, since no one could check the proliferation of bootlegs into Macedonia, and there was an enviable collection of vintage films. So, whenever the store had a slow day, Hari would watch a movie; most often an award-winning psychological drama or a relaxing comedy.

Westerners often had difficulty understanding how anyone at her age of thirty-five could still live with their mother, but such was the situation in Macedonia. Young people simply could not save enough from their humble paychecks or set aside money for rent and independent living. The small apartment had been paid off a long time ago, and they didn't have to worry about mortgage payments. Hari spent at least half of her salary on bills and food. The rest she spent on going out to cafés and restaurants; on her high-quality, sexy, but not too expensive, wardrobe; on make-up, perfumes, costume jewelry, magazines; and of course, on books. She bought literary fiction by the world's best-selling authors, such as Paulo Coelho, Haruki Murakami, Wei Hui, Banana Yoshimoto and Melissa P. She was not interested in the cheap and fluffy "bestsellers". On nights when she didn't go out, or when she suffered from insomnia, she would read with great zest.

Her brother, who was two years older, was a renowned architect and had moved away ten years ago with his wife to London. Her two nephews were born there. Now, they all lived in the Hammersmith neighborhood of southwest London.

She didn't remember her father. Her mother never – not even once – had shown her a photo. Her father was Greek, and his entire family lived in Greece. Hari had no contact with her father's side of the family. Long ago, he had come to Skopje to study architecture. Her mom never answered her question when she asked why he hadn't enrolled in Athens or Thessaloniki. Her mother was originally from a well-to-do merchant family in Veles, Macedonia. She had many relatives and usually spent her summers there.

Hari was only six months old when her father turned to her mother and said, "I don't want to live with you anymore."

Her mother was silent.

"Forgive me, if you can," he added.

Tears quietly rolled down her face, drying up on her cheeks that burned with disappointment. "I can understand you don't want to be with me anymore. What about the children?"

Without saying anything more, her father left. He wasn't a bad man, but deeply inside, he felt he would never be happy if he stayed with her, and the children had nothing to do with that, nor could they be of any help. And so, since that year of 1969, they never received any letters or postcards, not a single word, not one gift for Hari or her brother.

Her mother never said anything about him — neither good nor bad. She suppressed her emotions deeply and never gave into provocations from her kin. They seemed ridiculous with their phony sympathy. "Why would anyone find my life interesting," she would say, cutting the conversations short.

Her mother had spent her career working as a booth clerk at the main post office building. Her pay wasn't that high, but it was enough to provide a decent life for her children.

In her blue moments, she would remember the

poem "Bullfighter" by her favorite Macedonian poet, Blaze Koneski:

> *I have waited for so long for a single kind word,*
>
> *For someone to come and love me whole.*
>
> *O hatred, O bull. I've had enough years*
>
> *Of twisting your horn by my own hand.*
>
> *I'm getting weary of that mighty strain,*
>
> *And dull indifference creeps in my veins.*
>
> *O hatred, O bull, if I give up, regardless,*
>
> *Trample, trample me with your hooves.*

But she knew that she would not ever succumb to the negativity about Hari's father. Some family members found it strange that Hari's mother harbored no hatred for her ex-husband. She simply accepted her fate without lamenting.

**

Refreshed from the stroll through the city mall, Hari returned home with a bag of new socks. She had been trying to get rid of the bitter aftertaste of a fight with her mother; so, she had gone to clear her head. In moments like that, walking a few blocks to the downtown somehow seemed to help.

When she walked in, she could tell that her mother was not there. Hari opened the windows to allow for a draft as their apartment had no air conditioning. In the evening, the summer heat subsided. She went out onto the small terrace and noticed Martin standing in front of the shoe store down below, relaxing with a smoke.

"He said he quit smoking. So much for character," Hari thought.

He was a dear friend, and they would often drink coffee at his shop.

She liked the solitude on the balcony, watching passersby bustle calmly through the street below. She felt a strange longing for her brother, although they had never been particularly close. Within the past ten years, she had visited him in London only twice – when her nephews were born. She kept their pictures in her room and at the movie rental store.

Her mother's words still rang in her mind from their fight that afternoon: "You have no idea, not by a long shot, what it means to be single in life."

Hari had an irrational fear of marriage, and whenever her mother pressed her, she would spare no words to defend herself.

"Don't look at my life. Maybe you'll have the most wonderful marriage," her mother had said.

"I'm not thinking about it yet. I'm young. Got my whole life before me. I'm in no rush…"

"You're young? Who do you think you are?"

"You're not going to make me feel bad for being single and without children at the age of thirty-five. Like you made such great choices in your life, and now you want to share the wisdom?"

Her mother shot her a furious gaze, hissed something through her teeth, and slammed the door hard behind her. And that was the end of their fight.

Hari knew that when her mother returned home, they'd both act as if nothing had happened.

"We know how to forgive each other," she thought, mentally reconciling their differences, as she got up from the little stool on the balcony. She was in no mood for going out that evening.

"I'll make some french fries. Mom loves them," she thought.

It was eight in the evening. From the street, there arose the usual rattle of shops closing for the day, the shop owners preparing to go home.

**

As she turned on the computer, she noticed a letter from Manuel, whom she affectionately called

'Manu'. Ever since their relationship had begun, checking her e-mail had become a special ritual for her. Hari wasn't one of those folks who was unable to imagine their lives without computers, and she didn't spend that much time surfing the internet. She used it for sending and receiving mail and for typing the final versions of her novels. Otherwise, she wrote everything by hand. Many people were shocked to hear that, but their reactions didn't bother her in the least. Even the famed Macedonian writer Petre Andreevski wrote his books by hand; he had told her that himself.

Once she was having coffee with her favorite novelist Bozhin Pavlovski at the Barcelona café, and, rubbing his knuckles, he told her, "I always write by hand. My hands hurt from so much writing and correcting." She admired Pavlovski in many respects. His book "A Novel for My Departure" was her bible. She read it and reread it because it gave her special strength. Pavlovski was one of the rare writers who made it big out of the borders of Macedonia. He had a wonderful career as a publisher and writer there, but his success started to bother many in the writers' circles. False accusations about how Pavlovski plagiarized parts of his books from less known writers, began to appear on a regular basis in the daily newspapers and literary magazines. It soon occurred to him that there was a deliberate attempt to tarnish his reputation by other writers and publishers in an organized way. Therefore, he decided to leave Macedonia for good. After a one year stay in the United States, he settled in Australia, where he continued to thrive in the publishing and writing business. People who attacked and accused him back home, were long forgotten. In reading his book, Hari strongly felt that there is hope and opportunity for the writers to succeed abroad, particularly those that did not feel comfortable with the petty envy that prevailed in Macedonia amongst the writers' community.

Acknowledgements:

I would like to express my deepest gratitude to my husband. He is my biggest inspiration and my soul-mate; he has been there for me at every step in my life and wishes to see me happy always. I love you from here to eternity.

My sister Katya, whom I trust the most when it comes to my writing and all the important things in my life. A person who is beautiful inside and out, and the best sister in the whole world. You have always been my best friend and I love you from the bottom of my heart.

My parents, who are the most wonderful, good-hearted and non-envious people - they have taught me the values of life with their own example.

My nephew Goryan and my niece Sara, two golden souls, who inspire me to become a better person every single day, and with whom I long to be together forever.

My editor Eric Berlin, who respects my talent and does his best to let it shine.

Rebecca Dalton (www.RebeccaDalton.net), who formatted the book, and consulted with me about the different aspects of self publishing. She has helped me all the way with her indispensable insight.

To James (www.GoOnWrite.com), who designed the book cover and left everyone in awe because of the beauty of it.

To my stepdaughter, who has always been supportive of my dreams - she believes in me, she is my sweet friend, and has nice words all the time about my writing.

To Suzana Pandurska, Frosina Dramicanin, Anica Pop Trajkova, Tanja Velkova, Igor Pop Trajkov, Violeta Djoleva, and so many of my beautiful friends who are like angels sent from the heavens.

Ana Shapkaliska is a scriptwriter, novelist and short story writer from Macedonia, Southern Europe. She has worked in the TV Industry and accomplished many feature TV movies and feature serials, (based on original and adapted screenplays), as well as documentary movies. Many of her projects got awarded at several European TV Festivals. Her novel, "Govinda, Anuttam and the Juhu Temple" was published by TRI in 2005 in Skopje, Macedonia. Her story, "Thuraya's World" received the Short Story Award for New Writers (Honorable Mention) in Glimmer Train's September/October 2016 issue. She lives with her husband in Cary, North Carolina.

www.AnaShapkaliska.com | govilila@yahoo.com

Made in the
USA
Columbia, SC